FULL CIRCLE

PROPHECY OF AXAIN, BOOK 3

STEVEN ATWOOD

ISBN 13: 9781949788075

Published by Dragons & Lasers Press

Carrollton, GA 30116

CHAPTER 1

$\mathcal{E}$ven as the midday sun rose in the sky, the thick fog remained stubborn, hiding all of its secrets from the casual onlooker. Galin V Ravenward was riding next to his bride of six months. He'd grown into a strong young man, skilled in both combat and dragon magic. His plain clothes didn't let on that he was the rightful heir to the throne of Axain.

Her long, blond hair was pulled back into a ponytail. The tattoo on the back of her neck was a full moon depicted in gold, symbolizing the goddess Odella, whom she worshiped. Her blue eyes twinkled. "Are we going the right way?" She wore green robes embroidered with golden thread.

Galin smiled. "Of course."

"That's what you said last time," a male voice said behind them.

Galin turned around. "But, I'm sure . . . this time."

Ellis grinned. "Sure." He was a stout young man with short black hair and hazel eyes. Ellis wore a tan tunic with his daggers hanging from his belt.

The young woman with long red hair and a well-defined chest rode next to Ellis. Her eyes never left him. "Don't mind him," Mae said.

Jena giggled. "Let them be."

The hooves of Thea, Galin's mount, began to sink in the moist ground. The knee-high quagmire covered the ground like a thick rug. Galin shivered as a cool wind passed through his dark-blue tunic. His ears perked up as he heard a woman's scream through the fog. His eyes widened, looking at Jena. "Come on!" He cracked the reins. Thea galloped into the mist.

As they passed through the thick fog, a small house came into view. It had a thatched roof and the walls were made of logs, not boards. There was a man in black-clad armor with his shield hanging over his back. On the shield was a symbol. It had a tan circle surrounding a red crescent moon on the left with a lightning bolt on the right. In the center was a sword hanging over an olive branch. Galin frowned. That was the symbol of the Darkstriders. Those treacherous bastards aided Kade the Usurper in killing his parents and taking the throne. The knight was holding the reins of three horses. Where were the other two? They must have been inside. Doing what?

Another scream came from the small house. "Stop, please stop!"

Galin bore down and Thea charged at the knight. Before the knight even turned around, Thea trampled him underfoot. Galin jumped down with his sword drawn.

Jena and Ellis joined him.

"Mae, watch our back!" Galin said. "They may have friends."

Mae nodded.

Images of pain and torment raced through Galin's mind. He willed his rage to come to the forefront of his mind. A small tingle tickled his heart. It spread throughout his body like a virus. Tiny arcs began to dance across his skin. They ran down his arms to his hand to his sword. It began to glow.

"Ready?" Jena asked.

Galin nodded.

Jena flew to open the door.

Galin rushed inside. An unconscious male dwarf lay bleeding on the floor. Across the room, there were the two Darkstrider knights, tearing at the female dwarf's clothes like rabid dogs. Galin kicked one in the ribs, knocking him over. He skewered the knight with his sword.

Ellis jumped on the other's back and slit his throat with his daggers. He pushed the dying knight off the dwarf.

Jena knelt down next to the female dwarf. Blood was splattered across her beard. She was shaking. "It's okay. It's over now. What's your name?"

"Dunelin Kegbrow," she said. "What about my husband?"

"Are you hurt?" Jena asked.

"What about my husband?"

"Let me look." Jena moved over to the male dwarf. "What's his name?"

"Formoir, Formoir Kegbrow," Dunelin said.

Jena brushed his long, brown hair from his eyes. "Formoir, can you hear me?"

He said nothing. He didn't even move.

"Can you help him, Jena?" Galin asked.

Her hand ran down his arm until she felt a sharp bone sticking out of his arm underneath his shirt. She pulled back his eyelids and frowned. "He's got a broken arm and he's unconscious." She nodded. "Yeah, I can help him." Jena reached inside her robe and pulled out a small pouch. She placed a small bowl filled with incense near Formoir's head. Jena touched his arm and closed her eyes. "Min touch Helbred nom." A warm glow began to emanate from her touch. "Min touch Helbred nom." Formoir's body glowed, only for a moment. "Min touch Helbred nom!" Jena screamed as her arm broke and the bone forced its way through her skin. Blood began to pour out of her left arm.

Dunelin jumped back. "What black magic is this?"

"She's healing him," Galin said as he knelt down next to Formoir. "Wake up, come on, wake up."

Jena struggled to her knees, bowing her head in prayer.

"What's she doing?" Dunelin asked.

Galin smiled. "Healing herself."

"What—what happened?" Formoir said as he opened his eyes. "Dunelin?" Relief fell over his face as he saw his wife.

Dunelin rushed over to him. "You're all right!"

Formoir hugged his wife. "Will the one who healed me be all right?"

Jena's body glowed and then the pain was gone. "I'm good." She smiled at the dwarf. "I'm glad you're all right."

"I'm sorry we didn't get here earlier," Galin said.

Formoir and Dunelin stood up. "I'm glad you came," Formoir said. "Those bastards ravage the countryside and the king does nothing."

Galin raised an eyebrow. "Is he close? We're trying to find him."

Dunelin sniffed. "What for? Unless you have a lot of gold, he won't even talk to you."

"I have to try."

"Who are you?" Dunelin asked.

"I'm Galin, and this is Jena and Ellis. We're from Axain."

"You're a long way from home."

Galin nodded. "Yes, but we need to help end that," he said, pointing at the two dead knights. "They murdered my family, and many others. I'm going to put an end to them."

Formoir shook Galin's hand. "We are forever in your debt. Is there anything we can do to help you?"

"Tell us where the castle is so Galin doesn't get us lost again," Ellis said.

Galin frowned.

Jena giggled.

Formoir nodded. "Go northeast for two days, you can't miss it."

"You'll pass through Oakenhost," Dunelin said. She bit her lip.

"What is it?" Jena asked.

Formoir glared at his wife. "You won't like what you find there."

"What?" Galin asked.

Formoir couldn't look into Galin's eyes. "Not all dwarves treat humans . . . well."

"We'll be careful," Jena said. "May Odella bless you."

"Good-bye," Dunelin said.

Galin, Ellis, and Jena went back outside, where Mae was still standing guard. "Everything okay, sire?" Mae asked.

Galin climbed up on Thea. "We know where the castle is."

"Great," Mae said as she mounted her horse.

"What do you think Formoir meant by not treating humans well?" Jena asked.

Galin shook his head. "I don't know. But we're going to find out." He cracked the reins, urging Thea towards Oakenhost.

AFTER AN HOUR's ride along the empty dirt road, the outskirts of Oakenhost came into view. The horizon was cluttered with short stone structures behind a wall. Row upon row of tents were just outside the town. Smoke from a large cooking fire rose from the center of the encampment. On the road just outside of the camp were three large wagons. Dwarves with whips were forcing the humans to load up smoked beef into the carts. Galin frowned at Jena. "Let's go."

"Wait, Galin, we don't know what's going on here," Mae said.

Galin and Jena rode right up to the carts. "What are doing?" Galin demanded. A small red-haired dwarf with brown eyes frowned at them.

Jena gasped. "Oh, Galin, look!"

His eyes looked down at the humans' feet. They were all in shackles. Not enough to keep them from escaping, but definitely enough to slow them down. "Why are they being held as prisoners? What crime have they committed?"

The dwarf grinned. "Just being human." He raised his whip. "You'd better get down from those horses and join them, or else."

Ellis laughed. "Are we supposed to be afraid of you? A dwarf?"

"Are you taking their food?" Galin demanded.

"None of your damn business!" The dwarf motioned towards the other dwarves. "We've got trouble."

A slender woman with brown hair threw her meat into the cart and looked right at Galin. "Nurgurd, let them be. They are not with us."

Nurgurd glared at her. "They're human! The arrangement was for *all* humans, not just you. Sarah, mind your own business." He smiled. "I wouldn't want it to add more time to your obligation."

Galin blinked. "What arrangement?"

Ignoring Galin, Sarah motioned towards the town. "You've got your payment, now leave us alone."

Nurgurd nodded. "If they're here tomorrow, they share in your hardships. Understand?"

Galin watched the dwarves climb onto the carts. What was going on? How could dwarves overpower the humans like that? Especially when the humans outnumbered them?

Sarah nodded and the dwarves headed back to town. She looked right at them and frowned. "What are you doing here? It's not safe for our people. Come on."

Galin, Jena, Mae, and Ellis tied their horses off to the hitching post and followed Sarah into Tent City. He pinched his nose as the odor of people who hadn't bathed in months surrounded him. The tents were simple tepees, all around an enormous fire in the center. Not too far from the fire were four smokehouses hard at work. Heads peered out of their tents and their eyes softened. Galin exchanged worried looks with Jena. If dwarves treat humans like this, why would they help them? Perhaps, the prophecy was wrong. Perhaps, he was on a fool's quest after all.

A large man with grayish-brown hair and worn clothing stood up. "Who are these people, Sarah? They shouldn't be here."

Sarah took her place next to him, holding his hand. "My love, I couldn't let the dwarves take them."

The man looked at Galin. "Please, join us by the fire. I'm Jason," he said as he sat back down, with Sarah at his side.

Galin and the others promptly sat next to them. "I'm Galin V of Ravenward."

Jason blinked. "I thought the prince was dead. He died when Staerdale Castle fell, years ago."

"I was saved at the cost of many lives." He looked into Jena's eyes. "Sometimes, the cost was nearly too much to bear."

"I see," Jason said with a grin. "I know that look. I share it with my wife."

Jena beamed at Galin. "We just got married six months ago."

Ellis rolled his eyes. "We know, Jena. How many times do you have to keep telling us that?"

Mae hit Ellis in the shoulder.

"Ouch!"

"Be respectful," Mae said.

Galin glared at Ellis before turning to Jason. "Jason, why are you all in chains?"

Sarah looked away.

Jason sighed. "It was because of our parents. When the Darkstriders took over Axain, they cleansed entire villages of anyone they thought may be a problem. Former knights, squires, artisans, you name it. My father told me that he believed the Orcs just loved killing humans. The men were murdered, but what they did to the women and children was far worse."

Galin lowered his eyes. "I saw some of it in Drusas," he looked up, "before I liberated it."

"I—well—let me finish. Our parents loaded us onto a caravan and came here. At first, the dwarves welcomed us with open arms. Then, some of them didn't think it was fair to share pastures with their livestock. Some even went as far as attacking our settlement. You see, we used to be inside the walls."

Jena leaned in. "What happened?"

"There was an election about ten years ago. Stilgar Axfoot was one of those running for mayor of Oakenhost. He promised to rid Oakenhost of the humans, sending them outside the walls. Their troops rounded us up and threw us out. Our parents agreed to twenty years of servitude if they wouldn't send us back to Axain or turn us in to the Darkstriders," Jason said. "They occasionally do work for *them*."

Galin nodded. "I know. A group of dwarves attacked us north of Crey Village."

"Where?" Jason asked.

"My home." Galin's eyes softened. "You don't have to do this. Things are changing. That's why we are here. We're on our way to Croft Keep, to see the Dwarven king."

"For what?" Sarah asked.

"To seek an alliance."

They all laughed. "They'll never do that. Dwarves hate humans. Why would they jeopardize the business relationship they already have with the Dark-striders?"

Galin looked away. "I don't know. But, I have to try. We have an army building east of the Wailing Mountains right now. We are going to take back the kingdom."

Jena took Galin's hand. "Why don't you fight with us?"

Jason blinked. "I—" He looked at Sarah. "I don't know. We're not warriors."

"No," Ellis said, "you're slaves to four-foot-tall people for another ten years." He shook his head. "I don't know which is worse. Do you really want your children to be slaves, like you? What makes you think they'll even let you go in ten years? By that time, they'll be so dependent on you that they'll never let you go!"

Sarah's teary eyes met Jason's. "He's right." She touched her belly. "I don't want our child to be in chains, do you?"

Jason looked away. "Of course not."

"Well?" Sarah asked.

"Stilgar would never allow it," Jason said.

"How many people do you have?" Galin asked.

"Around eight hundred," Jason replied. "If you get him to free us, we'll join you."

Galin stood up. "All right, we'll go talk to them and try to make them see reason."

"They'll just lock you up," Sarah said.

Galin smiled. "I don't think so." He looked towards the town. With his dragon magic, nothing could go wrong . . . right?

ade Ravenward stared out the window onto Staerdale Castle's courtyard. His graying blond hair was unkempt and his once muscular body had turned into a flabby husk of an old man. His blue eyes sagged. All he'd ever wanted since his birth was to be king. Yes, his brother was the firstborn, but they were fraternal twins. Only a mere few seconds decided who ruled the kingdom until he killed his brother. He rubbed his eyes. Was it worth it? The endless nightmares and solitude caused him to ask that very question every time he saw the sunrise.

He sat down on the elaborate bed in the center of the room and sighed. The king's chamber was enormous. A tall table surrounded by polished oak chairs stood underneath a tapestry depicting his father on the far wall. Kade had two dressers, and his armor was displayed on a stand in the corner. Kade smiled as his eyes wandered over towards his old armor. How long ago was it that he could actually fit in it? With the Darkstriders in charge, being the king was more like a being a prisoner than a ruler. There was no power, none at all. He looked out the window. Maybe this was how the gods punish traitors.

"Kade, Tanyl wants you," Daylor said as he entered the room. His blue skin glistened in the sunlight, but his eyes were dark and lifeless. His red robes trailed behind as he approached the bed. "You've got to get over this—attitude of yours."

Kade glared at him. "Attitude? Hardly. I'm a prisoner here. I think that warrants some . . . hostility."

Daylor put his arm around Kade. "Look, I'm not Tanyl. I'm your friend, aren't I?"

"I guess." Kade returned to the window.

"What is it this time? Are you still dreaming about them?"

"My family?"

"Yes."

Kade looked back at Daylor. "Yes, I relive the day

I killed my brother's family every night. I relive that moment when I found out that Beldroth was controlling me the whole time." He stared back out into the courtyard. "That was the day I lost my soul."

"No need to be dramatic."

Kade whirled around. "Dramatic? Every time I walk through the courtyard, my people turn their backs on me. Whenever I go to a tavern, I sit alone. Not even the Dark Elves want anything to do with me. I have no human advisers or knights to socialize with. I'm . . . I'm lonely."

Daylor frowned. "Stop feeling sorry for yourself. You got *exactly* what you wanted, the way you wanted to get it. All we did was—assist you in achieving your dreams."

Kade glared at him. "Nightmare, you mean."

"If you wish," Daylor said as he moved over to a dresser. He picked up a brush and tossed it to Kade. "Clean yourself up."

Kade started brushing his hair. "What does he want this time?"

"It's your nephew again."

"What about him?"

Daylor leaned against the dresser, looking right at Kade. "He's strengthening his army to the east.

Every day more and more volunteers come from Ithsein, Qrento, Yresa, Nia, Plaka, and Grurg."

Kade laughed. "Untrained peasants. Who cares? They'll scatter after the first one is slaughtered. Farmers and merchants haven't got the stomach for war, Daylor. You of all people should know that."

Daylor yawned. "My duties do not require me to fight, so I don't. That doesn't mean I don't have the stomach for it."

Kade tossed the brush back to Daylor. "If he's building an army, why does that concern me?"

"Tanyl is tired of waiting, and . . ." Daylor looked away.

"And what?"

"Our king, who is still in Setan, sent Tanyl a message."

What the hell was he talking about? Daylor was acting so . . . proper. "Spit it out already."

"Tanyl received his brother's head in a box with a note."

Kade blinked. "What did it say?"

Daylor grinned. "The prince's head or yours. Simple and direct. Needless to say, Tanyl is no longer worried about starting a revolt and he needs your help." He moved towards the door. "I'll see you in the Great Hall."

Kade tossed on a blue tunic with a red cape. Maybe this was the time for him to reassert his power over the kingdom. No, maybe he could set things right so he could forgive himself. He hurried out into the hallway towards the Great Hall.

KADE WALKED down the long stone hallway towards the Great Hall. What if he helped his nephew kick Tanyl and his clan out of Axain? Everything would be forgiven, right? If his nephew murdered his parents and stood by while the Darkstriders tried to kill him, would he forgive? He shook his head. No, not a chance. Once Galin controlled Axain, Kade would be strung up on the castle walls. Yeah, he couldn't let him win. But, could he help kill him? Should he?

Kade came the elaborately carved oak double doors. He pushed through them and went into the Great Hall. It was a long, rectangular room with pillars on each side and benches lining the side walls. Ahead were two thrones sitting on top of a dais. A large wooden table was in the center of the room, and three Dark Elves were leaning over it. "What do you want, Tanyl? I'm busy."

Daylor stood up and smiled at Kade.

Across the table from Daylor was Tanyl. His short, black hair had gray sprinkled throughout. He wore the purple robes of the king's adviser. His lifeless eyes blinked. "Come over here. I've got a job for you."

Kade clenched his teeth as he moved over to the table. There was a large map of Axain sprawled out on the table. Small figurines, representing friendly and enemy forces, were strategically placed on the parchment. "What's this?"

Ryul looked up. His bald head glistened in the torchlight. Wrinkles surrounded Ryul's eyes as if he hadn't slept for some time. Normally, his chain mail coat was shiny and oiled, but not anymore. No, he'd become completely unkempt. "A map, stupid."

"I know that," Kade said. He peered at the map. "What's the map *of?*"

Tanyl glared at him. "Your nephew's forces." He pointed at the figurines at Iron Fist Keep and east of the Wailing Mountains. "It's been six months since he took the keep and his army has grown immensely."

"Why don't you send Ryul there with his Feral Orc Division and take it? Daylor said that you got an"—Kade smiled—"encouraging note from your king. By the way, how's your brother?"

Tanyl's eyes flared. "I don't need you that much."

"Let me kill him, Tanyl," Ryul said. "I know a whole town full of humans who'd love to get their hands on him."

Tanyl shook his head. "No, we need him . . . for now."

"How reassuring," Kade said. "Again, what do you want?"

"What will he do next?" Tanyl asked.

Kade blinked as all three Dark Elves stared at him. "Umm, how would I know?"

"Because you're human," Ryul said as his face reddened. "Tanyl, I told you this was a waste of time. I don't need military advice from *him*, a traitor to his own kind."

Daylor frowned. "Tanyl wanted the opinion from a *successful* conqueror, Ryul. That's why he didn't ask you."

Ryul slammed his fist on the table, knocking over a couple figurines.

Tanyl stared right at Kade. "Well?"

Kade's stomach twisted. Should he tell them what he really thought and be responsible for killing his brother's son? The last child in the Ravenward family line? "Do you still think he's the one your prophecy talks about?"

Tanyl nodded. "Yes."

"How can you be sure, Tanyl?" Ruyl asked. "It's been years since the prince escaped, and the world's armies haven't come against us. That prophecy is not real."

"What does it say?" Kade asked.

Tanyl lowered his eyes onto the map. "The human boy-king that can wield magic without components or words will unite the humans, gnomes, and dwarves to destroy the children of Methos."

"Children of Methos?"

"The Darkstriders," Daylor explained.

Kade rubbed his chin. "Do you think he knows about this prophecy?"

"Yes," Daylor said.

Tanyl nodded. "Yes, our operative confirmed it before they took Iron Fist Keep. She was lucky to get word to us."

Daylor cocked his head at Tanyl. "How come I didn't know about this?"

"You don't need to know everything, Daylor. Understand?" Tanyl demanded.

Kade nodded. "A spy?"

"Yes. In fact, you knew her mother, Beldroth. Her name is Chalia. A great pyromancer, just like her mother. This was her first assignment after she graduated from Tadus School of Magic." Tanyl began to study the map again. "What do you think, Kade?"

They were actually asking him. Kade couldn't help but smile. But, should he? What the hell, he could only guess anyway. "Assuming the prophecy is correct, he'd have to go north to Shumnar and to Fozzgart."

"I can do this, Tanyl," Ryul said. "I'll raze every village from here to the northern coast. I'll find them. I swear."

"That would be foolish," Daylor said. "Surely, you would encourage more people to join his ranks. Is that really the wise thing to do?" He looked right into Ryul's eyes. "Or is that the knuckle-dragger thing to do?"

"I'll snap you like a—"

"Stop it!" Kade yelled. "You're worse than children. Daylor's right, you can't do that."

Tanyl rubbed his neck. "Our circumstances have changed, Kade. We need to find them now."

"Send emissaries to Croft Keep and speak with their king. These are dwarves; offer them crowns for my nephew. Let them find him for you." He slapped Ryul's shoulder. "You see? Easy."

"What about the army?" Daylor asked.

Kade shrugged. "Send Ryul to Nia and send reconnaissance patrols into the mountains. Even though you can't bring large forces through the mountains without passing through Iron Fist Keep, a squad could slip through."

"What would they do there?" Ryul asked. "A unit that small would get killed easily."

Kade grinned. "You're not attacking the castle, silly. You're attacking the people he's protecting. Draw them away from the keep. Force them to remain spread out until you're ready to strike."

Ryul frowned. "That—that might work."

"Good. Kade, you lead the Feral Orc Division. Ryul will be your general," Tanyl said.

"What?" Ryul demanded. "I'll never be subordinate to a . . . a . . . human."

"I'm not doing it, Tanyl," Kade said. "Find someone else."

Tanyl licked his lips. "You don't have a choice."

"I gave you some ideas, but I'll not participate in the complete destruction of my family. He's the last Ravenward alive." Kade pointed at Ryul. "Send your attack dog. I'm sure his heart would be in it." He started to walk towards the door.

"Where are you going?" Tanyl demanded. "Damn it, get back here!"

"I'm going to my chambers. Good night." He hurried out of the room. *What have I done?*

CHAPTER 3

The sweet smell of baking bread hit Galin as he rode into Oakenhost. Thea trotted along the cobblestone road. He looked around and saw dwarves everywhere. It almost looked like a village of children, but with beards. They were running in and out of the small stone buildings and merchant stalls that lined the streets. Intermixed among the dwarves were Vulwin Elves, Gnomes, and *humans*. He leaned towards Jena. "I thought they locked all the humans up."

Jena nodded. "That's what Jason said."

"Maybe they didn't tell us the truth," Ellis said.

Galin shifted in his saddle. "I don't think so."

Mae rolled her eyes. "He just said that they treat humans poorly, that's all."

"She's right," Jena said.

"Let's find a place to stay." Galin led them through the center of town. As they passed through the square, a two-story stone building with music flowing out into the street caught his attention. Above the door was a polished wooden sign that read *The Kracked Keg*. Two dwarves were asleep on the porch with empty mugs laying next to them. Galin smiled. "I guess this place will work." They tied their horses to the hitching post outside the tavern. A beautiful human woman stumbled out onto the street.

Ellis grinned. "My kind of place." He pushed past Galin and rushed inside.

Jena rolled her eyes. "He'll never change."

"I hope not," Mae said as she ran after Ellis.

Galin cocked an eye at Jena. "You think they're . . . ?"

Jena shook her head. "Not a chance." She took his hand. "Let's go before they get into trouble."

Galin's eyes twinkled. "Sure." He led them inside.

As soon as they entered the bar, pipe smoke hit them in the face like a rolling fog. Beyond the sea of dwarves, humans, and Vulwin Elves, a human woman tended bar on the far wall. Just to the left of the bar was a staircase going upstairs. Tapestries depicting battles and the dwarven gods decorated the walls. Long tables with benches lined the room. The lute player was on a small dais along the right wall.

Jena smiled at Galin. "I love the music."

Galin's heart began to pound within his chest. "Me too." He leaned in to kiss her.

"Oh please," Ellis said as he pushed them apart. "Can't you newlyweds wait until after you're in your room?"

Mae hit Ellis's shoulder. "Knock it off."

Jena giggled.

"Let's find a place to sit," Galin said as he scanned the room for an empty table.

"I'll get us some ale," Ellis added as he rushed to the bar, with Mae close behind.

Along the right wall, near the window, was the only small round table in the room. It almost seemed out of place. "Over there," Galin said as he pushed through the crowd.

"Are we going to be here long?" Jena asked as she sat down on a stool.

Galin's heart pounded and his throat went dry. "We . . . we have to be social, don't we?"

Jena bit her lip.

Galin swallowed.

"Here's your ale," Ellis said as he slid them across the table to Galin and Jena. He and Mae sat down across from Galin and Jena.

"It doesn't seem like Jason and Sarah told us the truth," Mae said.

Galin sipped his ale. "No, it doesn't. There are plenty of humans here."

"There has to be more to the story than they told us," Mae said.

"Do we still try to free them?" Ellis asked.

Galin's eyes wandered over towards Jena. "Let's worry about that in the morning."

Jena rose to her feet.

Ellis frowned. "Hey, I just got you some ale. Stay a while."

Mae's hand brushed against Ellis's. "Am I not enough company for you?" Her plain silver ring emitted a faint glow.

Ellis smiled. "We don't need them to have fun." He waved them off. "Go and do your nightly married thing. We don't need you tonight."

Galin laughed. "Okay, see you two in the morning." He led Jena upstairs to their room for the night.

THE SUNLIGHT POURED through the curtains and onto Galin's face. He felt the warmth of his naked bride snuggled next to him. He loved being married. He loved spending every minute with Jena. Nothing else mattered to him. Galin looked down at his sleeping future queen. Yes, she would make a great queen and help him to be a good king. Just the two of them; they didn't need anyone else. "Hey, we've got to get up."

Her eyes opened with a coy smile. "We can wait a little while longer, can't we? The mayor won't see us first thing, you know." She smiled as her hand began to wander under the sheets.

"I guess you're right." He kissed her. Marriage was great.

TWO HOURS LATER, Galin and Jena wandered downstairs into the tavern. Ellis and Mae were sitting having breakfast at one of the long tables.

"Look," Galin said, "they can't take their eyes off each other."

Jena smiled. "I know."

Galin and Jena sat across from Ellis and Mae. "Have a good time last night?" Galin asked.

Ellis grinned.

Mae blushed.

"They did," Jena said.

"Would you like some breakfast?" a human girl asked. She was just a hair over five feet tall with brown hair.

"Please," Galin said.

"And you?" she asked Jena.

"Yes."

"Just be a moment." The waitress hurried away.

"How are we going to handle the mayor?" Mae asked. "We can't tell them who you are. It's too dangerous."

"She's right," Jena said.

"Here you are," the waitress said as she slid overflowing plates in front of Galin and Jena.

"Thank you," Jena said.

Galin tossed a fork full of scrambled eggs into his mouth. "We have to tell them, eventually. How can we get allies if we don't?" he said after he'd chewed and swallowed.

"Save that for the king," Mae said.

Is she right? Galin asked himself. Sure, ever since they took Iron Fist Keep he had been less . . . concerned about people knowing his true identity. Why not? The Darkstriders had no doubt now, right? The stories about Stilgar Axfoot didn't appear to be entirely true. Perhaps there was another side to the story that Jason and Sarah weren't aware of. Maybe? Galin nodded. "You're right."

AFTER THEIR STOMACHS WERE FULL, Galin, Jena, Ellis, and Mae walked through the small town. Dwarf children played in the street with their mothers chasing after them. No one yelled or swore or threatened Galin. Were Jason and Sarah wrong? Maybe. There had to be more to the story than perhaps even they realized.

As the group reached the edge of town, the mayor's home came into view. It was just like the waitress had said in the Kracked Keg. Large jewels were embedded in the gray granite walls. The decorative shutters were open and the gold lace curtains blew through the breeze going in the windows. A large mahogany door had a gold doorknocker that matched the handle. Galin swallowed. *Stilgar Axfoot must have more crowns than most nobles.*

Ellis's jaw nearly dropped to the ground. "Do you know how much one of those jewels are worth?

Jena glared at him. "Ellis, don't!"

Mae's hypnotic smile disarmed Ellis. "Our mission first, then . . . maybe?"

"No," Galin said. "Absolutely not. We're here for a reason, not for petty theft." He approached the door and knocked.

Ellis shrugged his shoulders. "It's not *that* petty."

The door swung open and a dwarf with long, brown hair and a beard down to his belly button stepped outside. "What do you want?"

Galin swallowed. Should he tell him? Jason and Sarah know, so—why not? If he doesn't know now, he would real soon. "I bring news from Axain. May we come in?"

The dwarf looked over Galin, Jena, Ellis, and Mae for a moment. He bit his lip. "No. Good day." He stepped back and started to close the door.

"But—" Galin began.

Ellis pushed past Galin and put his foot in the door, stopping it from closing, and stared right at the dwarf. "We really need to talk, *now*."

Galin blinked. He'd never seen Ellis act like that before. Ellis was almost acting like a . . . Dark Elf. He pushed Ellis out of the way. "Please, sir, we mean you no harm."

The dwarf extended his hand to Galin. "I'm Stilgar Axfoot. Come in."

Galin scowled at Ellis as he stepped inside. As he passed through the door, the odor of baking muffins made his stomach growl, even though it was full. They smelled that good! The large room had an elaborate woven rug on the floor, in the front of the fireplace. Two oversized, puffy, chairs sat next to one another with a small table in between them. There were two matching couches facing the table in the center. Tapestries and paintings decorated the walls. Across from the fireplace was the entranceway to the kitchen.

"You have a very nice home," Jena said.

"I'll get some tea. Please, have a seat," Stilgar said.

Ellis plopped down into the left chair and dust flew up in his face. "Damn," he said as he waved the dust cloud away

"I don't think you should sit there," Mae said. "Please, Ellis."

Galin motioned towards the couch where Mae was sitting. "Come on, Ellis."

Ellis shook his head. "I'm fine. Leave me—"

"No one sits in that chair!" Stilgar yelled as he came back into the room with a tray full of tea. "That's my wife's chair. Get out of that chair or get out of my house!"

Ellis jumped up. "Sorry, don't have an ogre over it." He sat next to Mae and smiled. "Sorry, sir."

"It's all right," he said as he put the tray on the

table between the couches. He took a cup and sat in the chair on the right. "What news is there from the south?"

Galin sipped his tea. "A revolt is happening, right now, as we speak."

"So? Why should I care?"

Jena leaned forward. "Why are those poor people outside the village in chains?"

Galin frowned at her.

Stilgar leaned back. "Is that why you're here?"

"In part, but let me—"

Stilgar waved him off. "It's okay. After the Darkstriders took Staerdale Castle, they began to slaughter any human that was a knight or a noble." He sipped his tea. "So, they came to Shumnar. We welcomed them for a time. Everything was fine for years. But then, they took the best grazing lands and the most fertile areas for their crops. When we went to talk to them about it, they simply told us that they were nobility and knights and didn't have to listen. Naturally, that got the people upset."

"Was that when you ran for mayor?" Jena asked.

Stilgar shook his head. "Just before."

"Let him finish," Galin said.

"About that time, the Darkstriders came north. They didn't make it this far, but the rumors about what they were doing to the dwarves on the outskirts was . . . horrifying. My wife and I couldn't let that happen to our people, so I ran for mayor. After I won, I spoke with the human leaders and told them what was happening. They agreed to move outside the town. Only two weeks or so later, the Darkstriders, led by Ryul, a Dark Elf general, camped outside of Oakenhost. The humans saw it before we did. They put shackles on everyone to make it appear that they were our prisoners. So, when the Darktriders came, Jason's father told them that they were my slaves." Stilgar's eyes began to well up. "Ryul didn't believe him. He questioned me about it. He stabbed my wife to make sure I was telling the truth. As they left, I held her close to my heart as she died. I kept my promise to her to keep the humans safe."

Ellis frowned. "Why are they still in chains? That happened a long time ago, right?"

Stilgar nodded. "Yes, it did. But, the Darkstriders still come through Oakenhost." He looked away. "They have a patrol camped outside the camp to make sure that we were telling the truth. They have been there since my wife died. If I free them or bring them inside the city, that patrol will burn Oakenhost to the ground."

"How do you know?" Mae asked.

"The Feral Orc captain told me so," Stilgar said.

"Didn't the dwarf knights at Croft Keep help?" Galin asked.

Stilgar shook his head. "No. We are not valuable enough for the king. You see, dwarf stature is dependent on how much tribute they give to the king."

"That sucks!" Ellis said.

"What if we kill the patrol for you?" Galin said.

Stilgar smiled. "Then I'd bring them into the town and give you whatever you want."

"I could always use more troops. My army is getting bigger by the day," Galin said.

The dwarf pulled on his beard as if in deep thought.

"Where are they?" Mae asked.

"They have a camp due north, just inside the forest beyond the pastures." Stilgar looked over at the ax leaning against the wall in the corner by the fireplace. "I can't speak for the town, but I may join you. But, you'd have to convince the king first."

"That's why I'm here," Galin said as he stood up.

"Who are you?" Stilgar asked. "You seem to speak with authority."

"I'm Galin V of Ravenward, nephew of Kade the Usurper. I'm the rightful heir to the throne. We already control everything east of the Wailing Mountains and I am here looking for allies." He pointed to Jena. "This is my wife and future queen, Jena." Galin motioned towards Ellis and Mae. "And these are our companions, Ellis and Mae."

Stilgar grinned. "Okay, let me know when that patrol is dead and I'll help you, even if the king doesn't give me permission."

Galin shook Stilgar's hand. "I look forward to fighting by your side."

"Me too."

CHAPTER 4

*L*ater, Galin and the others rode north towards the forest. The poor pasture was rocky and unkempt. Long grass swayed in the mild breeze, just above the horses' knees. On the far side, a line of trees, like troops in formation, outlined the pasture's boundaries.

Am I announcing my presence too early to them by killing this patrol? Galin thought. No, he already did that when he protected the dwarf family. Maybe he should just move on and head to Croft Keep? All he would get would be a few soldiers anyway, but only after the king agreed. If they kill this patrol, what's stopping the Darkstriders from sending another one? Nothing. But would they? Galin sighed. A person could go crazy worrying about this. His nose twitched. "Smell that?" Galin asked as he brought Thea to a halt.

"Fire of some kind," Jena said.

Mae nodded. "A campfire. Their camp must be in that wood line."

"Think they see us?" Jena asked.

Ellis rolled his eyes. "Why would they even be looking for us? We're in the middle of a cow pasture; of course they could see us. If it's even them. You're so—"

Galin glared at him. "Ellis, cut he crap. He's right though, *if* they're looking, they'd see us. I seriously doubt it. But, we can't go straight for them, either. They would know what we're up to." He urged Thea forward and veered slightly east. "Come on, I have an idea."

Was this going to work? It was true that every Darkstrider was looking for them throughout the kingdom, but Galin looked like common folk and his unremarkable features were easily missed. His gut twisted in his stomach, nagging him to reconsider. He was doing the right thing, wasn't he? No matter how hard he tried, he couldn't put that feeling out of his mind. There was no question that freeing those people was the right thing, but was he going about it the right way? Maybe ignoring it until the fighting was over was the best idea.

As they approached the wood line, Galin slowed Thea down. The breeze ran parallel to the line of tall pine trees. Galin swallowed. "Here we go," he said as he moved into the woods. Saplings, prickers, and ground cover decorated the forest floor. It was not impassable, but thick all the same. Galin tied Thea to a tree. "Let's leave the horses here."

Jena jumped down from Tyra. "How far away are they?"

"A few hundred yards," Ellis said as he slipped his daggers into their sheaths.

With his sword by his side, Galin moved in front of them. *Too late to turn back now*, he thought. "Let's go." Prickers scraped across his skin as he pushed through the underbrush. How many Darkstriders were there? Galin swallowed. He had no idea, none whatsoever. There could be one or five or a hundred for all he knew. Was he being foolish? Was this act really necessary to complete his mission in Shumnar? Maybe. Probably not.

Ellis moved close to Galin. "Want me to scout ahead?"

Galin nodded. He held up his hand, stopping Jena and Mae as Ellis scurried off towards the campfire.

"What's he doing?" Jena whispered into Galin's ear.

"Scouting the camp," Galin whispered back.

Jena bit her lip and stared into the woods.

She doubts me, Galin thought. His stomach twisted. Hell, he doubted himself. Why should she be any different? Sure, Ellis ran ahead and had even caused a diversion or two before, but something . . . feels different this time. Could his luck be running out? Sounds of crunching leaves was coming towards them. Galin raised his sword, waiting to confront the assailant.

Ellis emerged from the underbrush with a smile. As soon as he saw Galin with his sword raised, he frowned. "Did I piss you off that badly?"

"Sorry," Galin said. "I'm a little off today."

Ellis grinned. "Since when are you on your game?" He knelt down and brushed aside a few leaves covering the ground. He drew in the newly exposed dirt with his finger. "The camp is about two hundred yards ahead of us, here." Ellis jabbed his finger into the dirt. "To the south, about fifty yards, is the pasture we were on. They must camp there a lot because the underbrush is basically cleared."

"How many are there?" Galin asked.

"I counted eight," Ellis said. "Feral Orc warriors,

nothing else. Just like the checkpoint going towards Iron Fist Keep. They are eating around the campfire. It will only take them a second or two to attack, once they hear us." He patted Galin on the shoulder. "We're going to need that dragon magic of yours."

Galin nodded. "Let's pair up and spread out."

Jena drew her two short swords. "I'm with you."

Mae did the same. "Let's go, Ellis."

Galin rose to his feet. "Move out." He silently moved into the brush. With each step towards the camp, the smoke grew stronger. His heart beat faster. He looked over his left shoulder at Ellis and Mae twenty yards to the south. When they attack, the camp should divide up, right? Plus, they had the advantage of surprise. His ears perked up. The rumbling ahead was orcish, the language of the Feral Orcs. Even though Galin couldn't speak it, he did recognize it. He froze and listened. Laughing. Talking. Eating. Joking. No, they weren't onto them. He peered through the bushes to see the Feral Orcs gathered around the campfire, drinking ale or some alcoholic drink. *They're having a party*, Galin thought. The orcs swayed back and forth like they were . . . drunk. He looked to his left to see Ellis and Mae in the underbrush, waiting for Galin to make his move.

A Feral Orc let out a loud burp and rose from the campfire. With his eyes barely open, he grabbed his ax.

Galin watched the orc, with its ax dragging in the dirt, walk over towards the area where Ellis and Mae hid. *He's going to see them!* Galin thought. If he attacked Ellis now, all eight would converge on his lifelong friend and kill them both. Galin's eyes never left the orc.

The Feral Orc stood right over the bush where Ellis was hiding. He dropped his ax onto the ground.

Galin blinked. *What is he doing?* He watched the orc sway back and forth, as if he could fall over at any moment.

Ellis's eyes widened as he covered his face.

The Feral Orc let out a sigh of relief as he urinated on top of the bush where Ellis was hiding.

Galin covered his mouth, trying not to laugh.

"You bastard!" Ellis yelled as he flew out of the bush, knocking the orc to the ground. He thrust a dagger through the orc's right eye.

Galin envisioned Jena being captured by the Dark Elves and his rage exploded. Tiny arcs, like lightning, began to bounce across his flesh. When they danced from his hands to his sword, it began to glow. Galin charged at the orcs still sitting around the fire.

Seven Feral Orcs jumped to their feet with their axes in hand.

Mae let out a battle cry as she leaped at an orc. She swung her sword, aiming for its head.

The orc ducked and knocked away her sword.

She crashed to the ground as the orc raised its ax over her head.

Jena charged at another orc with both swords drawn. It tried to bat them away, but the orc was too late. Both short swords skewered the Feral Orc's chest. It crashed to the ground.

Three orcs barreled at Galin.

Think offense, Galin thought. He dropped to his knees and swung his sword at the three charging orcs. His glowing sword sliced through their legs as if they weren't even there.

The Feral Orcs screamed as they crashed to the ground.

Galin stood over them and raised his sword, putting them out of their misery.

"Mae!" Ellis snatched his dagger from the dead orc's eye and threw it at the orc standing over Mae. The dagger found its mark and buried itself in the Feral Orc's chest.

Galin looked around. "Weren't there eight?"

Ellis pointed at the two orcs racing into the woods. "Over there!" He started after them.

"Ellis, come back! Let them go," Galin said. "They're leading us into an ambush. Two orcs can't harm that village." He smiled at his blood-covered bride. "Everyone all right?"

Jena smiled at him. "Yes."

Galin smiled at Ellis, already rummaging through the Feral Orcs' camp. "Couldn't even clean yourself off first?"

"Nope," Ellis replied without even looking up.

Galin looked into the woods where the two Feral Orcs disappeared. *Was letting them go the right thing to do?*

AN HOUR LATER, Galin, Jena, Ellis, and Mae were riding back towards Oakenhost. Galin's gut twisted every time he reran the fight in his mind. Those two orcs that got away, why did he let them go? Was it the honorable thing to do? Absolutely. But was it the wise thing to do? What if he put the village in more danger by letting them go? What if—?

Ellis snapped his fingers in front of Galin's face. "Hey, wake up."

Galin frowned. "I was just—"

"Thinking, I know." Ellis grinned. "You're very boring when you're just thinking."

Small buildings came into view, just over the next rolling hill. "Let's camp here," Galin said.

"I thought we were seeing Stilgar," Jena said.

Galin nodded. "Ellis and I will ride ahead. We'll be back in half an hour, okay?"

Jena smiled. "Sure."

He glanced at Ellis. "Let's go." He led Ellis towards the village.

JENA WATCHED Galin and Ellis ride towards Oakenhost. "I hate watching him leave," she said as she pulled Tyra's feedbag from the saddlebags.

Mae started gathering up felled branches and put them into a pile. "Nothing is going to happen to them. I'll kill Ellis if he gets himself hurt." She grinned. "You can get Galin."

Jena laughed. "I know, it's just . . . I—we've had too many close calls." She watched Mae start the campfire. She loved Galin and he loved her, there was no doubt. When her mother was alive, she used to tell Jena how complete she felt when she had a child. Someone to teach . . . to mentor . . . to carry on the family tradition of service to Odella. Yeah, she wanted a child, but did Galin? Why would he? Jena swallowed. "How serious are you and Ellis?"

Mae smiled. "Very."

Jena plopped down next to the fire. "What are you going to do afterwards?"

Mae blinked. "After what?"

"The war."

Mae laughed. "The war has barely started. Why would I want to think that far ahead? I could be dead tomorrow' so could Ellis. Sure, I like being alone with him and he . . ." She blushed. "He knows what I like."

Jena cleared her throat. "I see."

"We can't be shy, Jena. Live for the moment; there may not be another." Mae pulled out a wineskin and held it up. "Want a swig?"

"Sure." Jena took a sip and handed it back. Should she talk to Mae about children? Her heart longed for someone to share her desire, but her gut screamed no. *What do I have to lose?* "Ever think about having children?"

Mae coughed as the wine went down the wrong

pipe. "What?"

"Kids? Do you want to have kids?" Jena bit her lip. Was talking to Mae about this a mistake?

"Um . . . Sure, why not?" Mae said. "Maybe, someday." She poured some wine down her throat. "What about you?"

Jena turned away. "I think so."

Mae leaned forward. "Aren't queens supposed to have heirs? I think it's a law or something."

Jena laughed. "No, that's not a law."

Mae eyes narrowed. "Well?"

Jena's lips trembled. She'd opened the door, she might as well step through it. It was too late to turn back now. "Yes, I want two, a boy and a girl."

Mae frowned. "Why? Do you think it is fair to bring up children in servitude? Life under the Darkstriders will never be anything more than that."

Jena's mouth dried up. "You don't think we're going to defeat them?"

"I—of course." Mae looked into the fire. "I guess I worry about the future too much. Why do you want a boy and a girl?"

Jena poked a stick into the fire. "The boy for Galin's heir, and the girl to become a priestess of Odella. The women in my family have been priestess for four generations and I want it to continue."

"What if she doesn't want to?"

Jena looked up at Mae. "I . . . I don't know. I never thought of that."

"Does Galin know?" Mae asked.

Jena shook her head. "No. Every time I start to talk about it, he changes the subject or puts it off till later."

"I don't get it. You two act like newlyweds, even after six months. You two never fight."

"No, we don't. I guess I'm ready for a baby and he's not," Jena said.

Mae grinned. "You're in control, not him."

"What do you mean?"

"Don't tell him. Get pregnant first, then tell him. What could he do about it?" Mae asked. "You only need one thing from him, girl."

Jena's face reddened. "I can't do that. It's not right." *This was a mistake.*

Mae shrugged. "I guess you don't want children that bad then, do you?"

"We're back," Galin said as he jumped down from Thea.

Ellis tied Runt onto a felled tree. "Miss me, Mae?"

Mae smiled. "You know I did." She leaped into his arms and kissed him.

"What's that for?" Ellis asked.

She smacked him. "Shut up and eat."

Whoosh. Whoosh. Whoosh.

Galin looked up.

Fear ran through Jena's soul as the hulking creature flew over them. It had great wings and gigantic claws that were only dwarfed by stories. Its blue skin glistened in the moonlight. It must have been at least thirty yards long. "What is it?"

"A dragon," Galin said.

Jena heart slowed down as the creature disappeared over the horizon. "It's fast."

Galin nodded. "Yes, it is.

"Head out first thing?" Ellis asked.

"Yeah," Galin said. "Me and Jena will take the first watch."

"Night," Mae said as she and Ellis cuddled next to the fire.

Jena's heart raced as Galin touched her hand. Should she ask him now? Why not? Surely he'd love the idea, right?

"Is something bothering you?" Galin asked.

Now, now was the time. Odella couldn't give Jena a better opportunity to talk about children. Yes, she was going to do it. As her mouth opened, her stomach twisted into knots. "No, nothing at all." Jena bit her lip. *I'm a coward!*

CHAPTER 5

Galin rode Thea down the dirt road towards Croft Keep as the midday sun sat on its throne high in the sky. Jena, Ellis, and Mae were all at his side. Galin smiled. He had been in Shumnar for only a few days and already he has doing good things for the dwarves. Surely, the dwarf king would see an alliance with them as an asset and nothing else. After all, what choice would they have? Surely, they wouldn't want to live under Darkstrider rule, right? Perhaps, they should—

Ellis snapped his fingers. "Hey, you in there?"

Galin blinked. "What?"

Jena giggled.

"Does he always do that?" Mae asked, trying hold back from laughing.

"All the time," Ellis said.

"Shut up!" Galin scowled. *What does he know anyway?* He stared straight ahead, ignoring Ellis. No more than a mile ahead, a stone wall began to appear over the crest of a hill. A castle with four golden towers stood high above the walls. "That must be Croft Keep."

Ellis rolled his eyes. "No kidding. How many other castles like this are there in Shumnar? Sometimes, you're just too stupid."

Galin glared at him. "What is your problem?" Galin's face reddened. "Where is this coming from?"

"Stop it, you two!" Jena yelled. "We're on a mission here. Act like it. Last one to the gates buys the ale tonight." She urged Tyra forward and raced towards the keep.

"Damn it!" Ellis chased after Jena.

"She's right, you know." Mae galloped towards the keep.

Galin stared at Mae. *Was her ring glowing?* He cracked the reins and charged after Jena.

The closer they got to the keep, the more elaborate it became. The walls were made of stone with diamonds, emeralds, and other gems embedded into them like an elaborate cloak on a barbarian's back. Galin was sure the temperament would be . . . similar. There was no moat or drawbridge, just an iron door with a thick portcullis. There were two dwarves wearing plate mail armor with short swords at their sides, checking anyone who sought entrance into Croft Keep. They must be in the dwarf king's army.

"A line to get in? Please," Ellis said.

Galin looked at the wagons, carts, and people waiting to go inside. They were from nearly every race, but no Darkstriders. Yeah, they came to the right place. He smiled. "Maybe they came to try to steal the gems from the keep walls."

"I bet they won't get caught." Jena grinned at Ellis. "Maybe you could get a few pointers."

Ellis laughed to himself. "Sure, right after you—never mind."

"What?"

"Forget it," Ellis said.

"Stop it," Galin demanded. "Focus! Let's go." He led them to the back of the line, right behind a gnome couple on a pair of ponies. They were short, like dwarves, but they had no beard and both were bald. Galin's eyes turned towards the dwarf guards checking every person. They were looking in saddlebags, poking through the carts filled with fruit, and questioning everyone. Was that normal? It seemed odd, at best. Why would a thriving kingdom, even during the Darkstrider rule over Axain, be that hostile towards its visitors? Surely they welcomed trade, like every kingdom, because of all the crowns they would raise in taxes. *Are they looking for something? Yes, they must be. But what? Us?* Galin's stomach tightened.

The two dwarves motioned the two gnomes to come forward. The one on the right stared right at Galin.

They are looking for us! Galin thought.

The other dwarf waved the gnomes along and approached Galin. "What's your business at Croft Keep?

Should he tell them the truth? Perhaps word from Oakenhost had reached his ears already. Galin swallowed. If he told them the truth, what's the worse that would happen? They'd be shooed away like a few stray mice. If he didn't, there would be no chance in forming an alliance. There was no choice. "I seek an audience with the king," Galin said.

The dwarf glared at him. "Who are you?"

"I'm Galin V of Ravenward. My parents were murdered by Kade the Usurper, who the stole the crown."

The dwarf on the right stared at him. "Weren't you called Seth Feran?"

Galin blinked. *How would they know that?* "Yes, when I was in hiding."

He put his fingers to his lips and let out a loud whistle. Twelve dwarves with their swords drawn stormed out the keep and surrounded them. "My cousin was with the expedition to capture you a few years back and you killed him with some kind of magic."

Ellis drew his daggers.

Mae and Jena looked right at Galin, as if waiting for orders.

"Put them away, Ellis," Galin said. He turned towards the dwarf. "What do you want?"

"Surrender and the king will see you." The bearded dwarf grinned. "He's been waiting for you."

"If I don't?"

"Then you won't see the king, we'll kill your friends, and sell you to the Darkstriders."

Galin looked at the dwarves. They could probably take them, but he wouldn't get the alliance that he needed. No, he didn't have a choice. "Okay."

"What?" Ellis demanded. "You're as crazy as a goblin pregnant with an ogre's baby."

Galin glared at him. "Just do what they say. We

have a mission to accomplish." He handed his sword to the dwarves.

Jena, Mae, and Ellis did the same. "I hope you know what you're doing," Ellis said.

Two more dwarves came out of the keep with four sets of shackles.

"What are you doing?" Galin demanded.

"Taking you prisoner," the dwarf said as he put the chains on Galin.

"We had a deal!"

"We do. You'll see the king . . . for sentencing," the dwarf said as he pulled Galin towards the gate.

He looked back at his loving bride. Tears were rolling down her cheeks. *What have I done?*

GALIN WAS DRAGGED through the town inside the castle walls towards the castle. The small buildings were made of wood with thatched roofs. Dwarven merchants lined the main street as if to harass travelers to purchase their wares. Smoke from the blacksmith's forge stung his nose. It reminded him of his adoptive father's shop back in Crey Village.

"We're nearly there," said the dwarf that was dragging Galin by his shackles.

As they turned the corner, the castle entrance came into view. The iron door was open and the portcullis was raised. Four dwarf guards wearing chain mail armor stood just outside the gate. "This way," a dwarf guard said as he led them inside.

Galin swallowed. Was it arrogance? Should he have been more careful? True, after his first victory at Iron Fist Keep, he hadn't hidden his identity. Why should he? How could he make an alliance in hiding? He couldn't. No, it wasn't arrogance. He had no choice.

After navigating through the corridors, they came to an elaborate set of double doors with the Stormtoe family crest carved into the wood. As they approached, the two dwarf guards opened the doors.

The throne room was enormous, with stone pillars spread throughout the room. They stood like silent guards watching over the kingdom. There was a blue rug with gold fringe on the polished marble floor leading up to the thrones. The throne on the left was larger, but they were both made of gold and decorated with diamonds and emeralds. An aging dwarf with gray hair and a long beard, wearing a flamboyant robe, sat in the larger throne. His queen sat next to him. She was plump, with a long, gray beard as well.

Galin blinked. Was that the life of a king? Would that be him and Jena one day? Well, without the beards.

"Is that them?" the king asked as he gazed upon Galin, Jena, Mae, and Ellis. He pointed right at Galin. "Is that Galin V of Ravenward? The ones the Darkstriders are so terrified of?"

The dwarf bowed. "Yes, Your Majesty."

King Luthur Stormtoe pulled out a monocle and put it into his left eye. "You don't look like much." He sighed and put the monocle back in his pocket. "Do you know the Darkstriders have a price on your head?"

Ellis grinned. "Whatever it is, it's not enough."

Galin stepped forward and raised his shackles. "Why are we in chains?"

"You're dangerous. We heard about you saving a family from some Darkstriders. For that, I thank you. I already sent word to Tanyl that he needs to . . . discipline his ranks," Luthur said.

"Tanyl?" Jena asked.

"He's King Kade's advisor, or puppet master. Whatever you like. Tanyl is the one really in charge." Luthur grimaced. "In truth, he rules us all."

"How?" Mae asked.

"The reason you don't see garrisons of Darkstriders here is because I give them no reason to install them. I pay his taxes and send my troops to do jobs for him from time to time," Luthur said.

"Dwarves tried to kill us in Crey Village. That was the first time I saw a dwarf. Was that one of those *jobs*?" Galin asked.

Luthur nodded. "Yes. The bounty on your head is now over 200,000 crowns."

Galin straightened up. "You could join us and help us fight them."

"Fight the Darkstriders? With what?"

"We already took Iron Fist Keep and control the lands east of the Wailing Mountains. The Vulwin Elves are with us too," Galin said.

Luthur snorted. "What's left of the Vulwin Elves, you mean. If what you say is true, why come here?"

"I'm seeking an alliance with yourself and the gnomes. To conquer Staerdale Castle, we need more assets than we currently have." Galin held up his chains. "Release us and join our cause. That way both of our lands can be free from the Darkstrider menace."

Luthur leaned back in his throne. "What's in it for me?"

Galin blinked. What did Luthur mean? Was freeing his people from underneath Tanyl's heel not enough? What would a dwarf want? His eyes gazed upon the gold throne. "When I sit on the throne of Axain, I'll give you free access to Port Eldham for one year." He bit his lip. Was that wise? Was he bargaining his kingdom away before he even had it?

Luthur tugged at his beard. "Tempting, but no." He grinned at Galin. "I'll take the 200,000 crowns now." He looked away. "I can't go against them. If any of their soldiers gets hurt, it has to be because they broke some law. There are several patrols in Sumnar, but no garrisons. I don't want that to change. I'm sorry you failed in your quest. I'll have you delivered to Tanyl in the morning." He motioned them to the door. "Take him to the dungeon for the night."

Several dwarf guards grabbed Galin's chains, pulling him out of the throne room.

Galin looked back at the empty throne. *What have I done?*

STILGAR WAS SITTING in his chair with the firelight from the fireplace dancing across his face. He sat down his fifth mug of ale onto the table in front of the couch. Yeah, it was one of those nights. He looked over at the matching cushioned chair next him. It had been empty ever since his beloved died. "One more mug," he said as he rose from the chair and headed towards the keg in the kitchen.

His eyes flashed towards the door as a woman screamed and then . . . it was gone, as if it was cut off. Firelight poured in through his windows, illuminated his house from the outside. "What the hell is going on?" Stilgar grabbed his ax and ran outside.

Tears rolled down his face as he saw Oakenhost on fire. It must have been at least two companies of Feral Orcs destroying everything. Dwarf men laid in pieces on the street like broken toys. The women . . . the women's flesh was torn from their bodies.

"Help!" a female dwarf screamed from around the corner of his house.

Rage filled Stilgar beyond anything he'd ever felt before. He raced around the corner.

A large orc was tearing the clothes off the dwarf woman, as if to rape her.

"Not in my town!" Stilgar charged at the orc, knocking it off the dwarf. He raised his ax and slammed it down, severing the orc's head from its body.

"Thank you," the woman said as she struggled to

get to her feet. She gathered her clothes and put them back on. "Thank you so much."

Stilgar motioned her towards the darkness. "Quickly, you've got to get out of here. Save yourself."

"What about you?" she asked.

"Never mind about me. Go!" He watched her run into the darkness towards the woods. At least he'd saved one dwarf. Was this his fault? Stilgar turned back towards the street, looking for more.

She screamed.

He whirled around. Stilgar's heart ached as he saw her head bounce across the ground towards him. "What have I done?"

"You betrayed your people, Mayor Axfoot," an orc's voice said as it emerged from the darkness.

"What do you want?"

It smiled. "Did you really think we only had one patrol out here looking after your village?"

Stilgar's face flushed as more orcs began to encircle him. "That's the only one I've ever seen." What could he do? Was this the end? In the afterlife, would he see his beloved wife again? Was he worthy after letting the town get ransacked by the Dark-striders?

The orc pulled out a dagger. "Maybe we should skin him?"

Stilgar's heart beat faster. The blood drained from his face. His eyes began to well up. "Please . . . don't." As soon as the orcs started to laugh, Stilgar charged the orc. As soon as he got close, he felt the dagger slam into belly, piercing his organs. Warm fluid began to pour out of his belly. His knees became weak and he crashed to the ground. "The king . . . the king will find out. Your deal with the dwarves will end. No . . . more . . . tribute to the Darkstriders." Stilgar reached his hand towards his belt, away from the orc's sight.

The orc leaned in. "Your treachery gives us a reason to take over your mines and murder your kind, like we did the humans."

"You . . . bastard. Come . . . come closer."

The orc laughed. "Last request? From me?" It leaned in closer. "What do you want?"

Stilgar's last surge of strength flowed through his veins. "To not go alone!" He tore his wife's dagger from his belt and slammed it into the orc's throat. "That was for my wife!" He pushed the dying orc off him. Spots . . . black spots appeared, filling up his sight. Stilgar Axfoot passed into the afterlife.

id they really get him? Kade thought as he raced through the corridors in Staerdale castle towards the Great Hall. He barreled through the double doors and burst inside. Galin was kneeling in front of Tanyl with his hands tied behind his back. "What's going on here?" Kade demanded.

Tanyl unsheathed his long sword. "You're finally going to be a real king." His thin lips twisted. "Anything to say to your soon-to-be-departed nephew?"

Galin stared right at Kade. "Uncle, please don't let him do this. Don't let our family name be destroyed. Where is your loyalty to *your* father?"

Kade blinked. Galin was taken from the castle when he was just a baby; how would know about

Kade's father? "Tanyl, don't. Let me . . . take him. I'll keep him under house arrest."

Tanyl glared at him.

"Please, Tanyl, the boy's right. He's the last of my family line." Kade's eyes began to well up. "I'll take care of it." His eyes widened as Tanyl raised his sword above Galin's head. "Don't!"

Tanyl's sword cut through Galin's neck, severing his head from his body.

Kade stared at his nephew's head as it rolled to his feet. He knelt down and picked up the severed head. Galin's eyes were closed. A tear rolled down Kade's cheek. "What have I done?"

Galin's eyes flashed open and glared at Kade. "Traitor!"

KADE LEAPED out of the sweat-soaked bed. Perspiration poured down his face as he looked around his bedchambers. The early morning sun crept in through the window. *That damn dream again!* Kade threw on a blue robe.

The door flew open and Daylor ran inside. "Are you all right? I heard you scream."

Kade smiled at the Dark Elf. Daylor was his only

friend. Was he the enemy? Sure, but so wasn't Kade, right? "Close the door, please."

"Sure," Daylor said as he closed the door. "Was it—"

"Yes. It was that damn dream again. I can't get it out of my head."

Daylor rubbed his chin. "Maybe you shouldn't."

Kade turned around. "How do you figure?"

"Sometimes, the gods use our dreams to communicate with us. Sometimes, they tell us what we need to do to fulfill our destinies."

"You sound like a priestess of Odella. Do you actually believe in that nonsense?" Kade asked.

Daylor nodded. "Where do you think magic comes from?"

Kade shook his head. "No idea, but that doesn't mean it comes from the gods. Even if it did, so what? Tanyl will never get my nephew and my family will continue."

"Why is that important to you now?"

Kade pointed to his face. "Look at me. I'm old. My dreams of becoming king came true, but the cost was too high." Kade sat down on his bed as his eyes began to well up. "I killed my own brother and his wife. I killed my fellow knights and enslaved my father's kingdom. I . . . I'm a traitor."

"No, you're not. Beldroth used her magic to control you. You were her puppet, nothing more." Daylor sniffed. "That's probably why you hid in here for so long."

Kade rubbed his eyes. "Maybe."

Daylor leaned forward. "What do you want?"

"I want to save my family and right the wrongs I've—I didn't say that," Kade said as the blood drained from his face.

Daylor rose to his feet. "Nothing to worry about. Even the Darkstriders don't execute people for their dreams; well, not yet anyway."

"You've always been a good friend to me, Daylor. Hell, you're my only friend."

Daylor moved to the door. "Maybe you should act on your dream." He closed the door behind as he left the room.

Kade blinked. *What did he mean by that?* He stared at the Ravenward family crest hanging on the wall above his bed. *I've got to do something. I've got to save my nephew.*

SUNLIGHT CREPT through the barred window, shining in Galin's eyes. He looked over at Jena, Ellis, and Mae sleeping on the stone floor. He swallowed. Was the prophecy wrong? Maybe he shouldn't believe in his own inevitability. He'd led his wife and best friend to their deaths. If he had his sword, he might be able to use his dragon magic to break out, right? Galin shook his head. No, no way. The cell was made of iron and rock. *Damn it!*

The heavy wooden door slammed into the stone wall as the door swung open. Six dwarves wearing chain mail armor hurried into the dungeon.

The guard leaped to his feet, giving the lead dwarf a sharp salute. "Good morning, Prince Riedel." He cut his salute. "What can I do for you?"

Riedel never took his eyes off Galin's cell, as if he didn't hear him.

Galin shook Jena. "Get up."

Ellis's foggy eyes blinked. "What's going on?"

Mae sat up.

Riedel pointed to Galin's cell. "I need them. My father demands to speak to them."

The plump guard waddled over to the cell and unlocked it. "You heard him," he said as he opened the door.

"Get them!" Riedel ordered the other dwarves.

Five dwarves rushed into the cell and yanked Galin and the others to their feet.

"Bring them to the king." Riedel led the group out of the dungeon.

Ellis frowned at Galin. "What did you do to piss them off this time?"

The dwarf dragging Ellis out the door smacked him in the back of the head.

"Ouch!"

Ellis's comment felt like a spear through Galin's chest. He'd failed them. *Did they say, 'bring them to the king?' Why the king? Why not the prison wagon to deliver them to Tanyl?*

AFTER BEING DRAGGED through Croft Keep by his shackles like a common criminal, Galin was tossed on the floor in front of Luthur. *Why am I back here?* Galin thought.

Luthur glared at his son. "Riedel, why are they still in shackles?"

Riedel's face went white. "Father, I thought . . ."

Luthur motioned to the guards. "Remove them, now!"

Five dwarves swarmed Galin, Jena, Ellis, and Mae, removing their chains faster than they were put on. It was almost as if they feared their king.

Ellis smacked a dwarf on top of the head as he

stood up. "You'd better run, before I call your babysitter."

Galin glared at him.

Ellis shrugged his shoulders. "What?"

Luthur cleared his throat. "Don't do that again, *human.*"

Jena held Galin's hand.

Her touch boosted his confidence. How can he fail when he has such a wonderful woman behind him? "Why are we here?"

"You lied to me," Luthur said.

"No I didn't."

"Not telling me the whole truth is still lying." Luthur looked away. "Even though I like what you did, as king I have to go beyond my own personal beliefs. I—"

"Need to do what's best for the kingdom," Mae said.

Luthur nodded. "Yes."

Galin's gut began to nag at his soul. He'd changed his mind . . . had to be. "Something happen?" he asked.

"I got word this morning that Oakenhost was burnt to the ground," Luthur said.

"The mayor?"

"There were *no* survivors." He slammed his fist

on the arms of the throne. "Those bastards impaled men, women, and children around the town. There must have been hundreds of them."

"How do you know?" Jena asked.

Luthur rolled his eyes. "Patrols, my dear. A patrol, on their way back here, went through the town early this morning and saw them."

"Are you sure it was the Darkstriders?" Galin asked.

"No doubt. Obviously, it was retribution for the Darkstriders you killed."

Galin's heart sank. *All those people died because he thought he was invincible and always right. Was he beginning to believe in the prophecy more than the Dark Elves?* "I'm sorry." He straightened up. "You were right the first time. Turn me over to them. Save your people. I . . . I won't cause more innocent people to be killed anymore."

Luthur jumped to his feet. "It's too late for that!"

"How so?" Mae asked.

Jena smacked Mae's shoulder. "You want Galin to die?"

"No," Mae said.

Luthur motioned over a servant wench as he sat back down. "Tea?"

Galin shook his head.

Luthur frowned. "Fine." He waved the dwarf away. "You've already dragged us into your foul war."

They're going to help us, Galin thought.

"If I don't react to the Darkstriders burning down one of our towns and impaling all the resident, I'll be strung up by my own knights. If I do react, I declare war on the Darkstriders. A war that I cannot win alone. I need an ally."

"I'm glad to have you," Galin said.

Luthur leaned forward. "What's the plan?"

Galin smiled. "Have an emissary meet us in Tarc in two moon cycles. Brock will meet us there. We are gathering allies from across Ceyceuna. We're going to overwhelm them."

Luthur frowned. "That's no plan."

Galin bit his lip.

"We can't tell you until you're there with your troops. You were going to turn us over just a day ago," Ellis said. "If the situation were reversed, would you tell us your plan?"

Luthur grinned. "Of course not. I'd wait until the very last possible moment."

"How many troops can you commit?" Galin asked.

"Ten thousand, including war mages and siege

equipment," Luthur said. "I want one thing in return."

"Name it."

"When you're king, I want some mining rights in Axain. The Wailing Mountains are loaded with gold and silver."

Galin grinned. "I'll consider it, after I'm king. All right?" Galin countered.

Luthur laughed. "You're going to be a great king. Are you heading there now?"

"No, we're heading to Croglang Castle in Fozzgart to seek an alliance with the Gnomes."

"Why?"

"They have flying machines," Galin said. "Why go through walls if you can go over them?"

Luthur nodded. "I like your thinking. All right, I'll meet you in Tarc two moon cycles from now." He looked at Riedel. "Return their belongings."

"Thank you, Your Majesty," Galin said as he bowed to Luthur.

"Get up." Luthur extended his hand to Galin. "Let's beat those bastards into the sea."

Galin shook his hand. "No, let's drown them in it. Axain will be ruled by my family again and we'll have peace."

Luthur's eyes began to well up as he smiled. "Aye, we will come full circle."

Galin took his sword from Riedel. "Farewell. I'll see you in Tarc."

Luthur waved at them.

Galin led them out of the throne room. *We did it!*

CHAPTER 7

Galin and Jena were riding side by side, with Ellis and Mae bringing up the rear. The cool breeze flowed through Galin's light-brown hair as they traveled east along the hard-packed dirt road. It was almost like Odella herself was congratulating him on another step closer to fulfilling the prophecy.

"How long will it take to get to Fozzgart?" Jena asked.

"Two weeks, I think," Galin replied.

"Ever think about . . . afterwards?"

"What do you mean?"

Jena smiled. "You know. After this is over and we are on our thrones in Staerdale Castle."

"Sometimes—well—yeah, I do." He looked over at his loving bride. "You're going to look so beautiful on the throne."

"You mean I'm not beautiful now!"

Galin blushed.

Jena giggled. "I'm kidding. What about an heir? Kings need an heir, don't they?"

An heir? What the hell was she talking about? Galin thought. "I guess."

"I'm looking forward to being a mother, someday. Are you?"

Galin smiled. "I can't be a mother."

Jena punched him in the arm. "You know what I mean."

"I would like to be a father someday. After the war is over and we've won. I don't want to bring a child into a world where it would be a servant to the Darkstriders," Galin said.

Jena touched her belly. "A child is not an it."

"You know what I mean." Galin grinned. "Besides, as soon as you have a child, all the fun stops."

Jena frowned. "It can stop even before I have your child."

"I see where this is going," Galin sighed. "I'm just

not ready, and I don't want to be a father for a long time. I'm sorry. Besides, why would you want to ruin what we have?"

Jena's eyes welled up. "Sometimes, life doesn't give us what we want." She cracked the reins, pulling ahead of Galin.

What did I do this time? Galin thought.

I'm not one of Tanyl's servants, Kade thought as he navigated through the hallways in Staerdale Castle towards the Great Hall. The two Dark Elf guards opened the double doors as he approached. Tanyl, Ryul, and Daylor stood around the long table in the center of the room. There was a map of Axain, Shumanar, and Fozzgart laying on top. Kade smiled as Tanyl pointed at something on the map. *They're stuck.* "Why have I been summoned?"

Tanyl looked up. "About time you arrived, Kade."

This new rebellious streak emboldened him. "I'm not to be called like some dog."

Ryul glared at him. "How dare you speak to Tanyl that way!"

Daylor put his hand on Ryul's shoulder. "Take it easy."

Tanyl rolled his eyes. "You two fight like children." His eyes narrowed. "Kade, come over here . . . please."

He's pissed, Kade thought. Ever since he'd killed his own brother, Kade had felt . . . regret. Was it regret or anger at his own stupidity? Sure Beldroth was controlling him with her ring, but that was no excuse. An accomplished prince and warrior should have figured it out before it was too late. Now, he stood at the precipice of either glory or damnation. It was obvious why they'd called him. Could he help them? No, he already promised himself that he would save his nephew. If not him, then who? There were over 500 humanoids in Staerdale Castle and he never felt so alone. Maybe—

"Kade! Get over here!" Tanyl yelled.

Kade smiled. "Of course. Sorry." His eyes wandered over the maps on the table as he moved next to the Tanyl. Small figurines were on top of the maps, signifying troop locations, possible enemy positions. It was a standard military map. "What am I looking at, exactly?"

"We don't need his help," Ryul protested.

Tanyl glared at him. "Do as you're told or I'll have you questioned by the seers."

The blood drained from Ryul's face. "No, Tanyl,

you . . . you don't have to do that." He cleared his throat, as if to hide his fear. "Kade, we have received reports from our outpost north of Tarc. There's trouble in Shumnar."

Kade's lips curled. "My nephew?"

Ryul nodded.

"I see." Kade tried to hide his smile. The Raven-ward family was always able to make the best out of the worst situations and, sometimes, come out ahead. His nephew was getting the results like his father. Was it possible for his nephew to forgive him for what he did? Would he? He rubbed his chin. "What's the situation? Not just in Shumnar, I need to know all of it."

"Galin not only controls everything east of the Wailing Mountains, but he's building an enormous army as well. Humans, Vulwin Elves, and even some Feral Orcs."

"Orcs?" Kade asked. "How?"

Tanyl spit on the floor. "He showed them . . . mercy. He's nothing more than a sniveling coward."

Kade gazed at Tanyl. He'd never seen him like that before, not in almost two decades. "Worried about your head in a box, Tanyl?"

"Shut up!" Tanyl said.

An opportunity, perhaps? Maybe he could use Tanyl's fear to his advantage? Kade focused on Daylor. "I heard Galin can use magic."

Daylor nodded. "Yes, a very old and powerful magic. One that doesn't need spell components or incantations. His emotions create the magic and determines their power."

"What do you mean?" Kade asked.

"Galin can kill with a touch. His sword can slice through flesh and bone without even stopping," Daylor said.

Tanyl frowned. "Stop talking like a damned seer, Daylor." His sagging eyes stared right at Kade. "His magic is very limited. Basically, it merely enhances his melee fighting. That's all."

"I see," Kade said. "If he's that weak, why do you need me?"

"I don't," Ryul interjected.

"I need your help to kill him," Tanyl said. "Not you, personally, but I need to know what his plan is."

Kade grunted. "Really? How am I supposed to know that?"

Daylor moved closer to Kade. "Look, Dark Elves and humans think differently, that's all. Tanyl spent years trying to find him and then trying to stop him. His failure reached our king." He smiled at

Tanyl. "I wouldn't want my friend to . . . lose his head over it."

"Touching." Kade leaned over the maps. "What do we know?"

Ryul pointed to the map of Shumnar. "He is in Shumnar, seeking allies."

"And?"

Tanyl sighed. "The dwarves sided with him. They had no choice and they knew it. After my rebellious patrol burnt down Oakenhost, the king had to respond. Any action like that would lead to war. I'd have done the same thing."

Kade shook his head. "Really? Just send a legion to Croft Keep and annex Shumnar into the kingdom. Are you really that cowardly?"

"He can't," Daylor said. "If we do that, we risk leaving Staerdale Castle unprotected and a vulnerable target for your nephew."

"You said he was in Shumanar."

"*Was* is the correct term," Tanyl said.

Kade blinked. "What do you mean?"

Tanyl shook his head. "They're gone. Our source has informed us that they're heading to Fozzgart."

"Source?"

"Beldroth's daughter, Chalia. She's keeping an eye on the . . . Situation," Tanyl said.

Daylor raised his eyebrows. "Really? Chalia?"

"You know her?" Kade asked.

Daylor bit his lip. "No, not at all. I . . . have great respect for her mother and father."

Kade slid the map of Fozzgart closer. "Why here?"

"The prophecy states that the human boy-king that can wield magic will unite the world against the Darkstriders," Tanyl said. "That includes those filthy, arrogant gnomes and their wretched machines."

Kade rubbed his chin. "I see you have a real problem on your hands."

Tanyl nodded. "Yes, but we have a solution. My seers have informed me that he must use dragon magic."

"Really? Dragon magic?" Daylor snickered. "Those fools will tell you anything to leave them be."

"They also said that there may be a way to nullify it or snuff it out altogether."

Daylor shook his head. "No, not possible. I'm familiar with dragon magic, and that cannot be done."

"They believe they can," Tanyl said.

"Why do you believe them?" Kade asked.

Tanyl smiled. "I told them I'd kill them if they're

wrong." He looked squarely into Kade's eyes. "That's why I need you."

"For what?" Kade demanded. "I won't help you kill my nephew. I just won't do it."

Tanyl tore his eyes away. "Fine. I'll kill you instead." He motioned to Ryul. "Kill him."

Ryul was practically drooling. "With pleasure."

Kade didn't flinch. "You can't kill me and you know it."

"Why not?" Tanyl demanded.

"There are more human knights than Dark Elf Darkstrider knights in Axain, especially in the castle. You'd also lose your human face to your invasion," Kade said.

"So?"

Ruyl stepped back.

Kade leaned in towards Tanyl. "If you lose Axain to a human revolt, the king will ship your head to your mother." He grinned. "Assuming she gives a shit about it in the first place."

Tanyl snarled at Kade. "How dare you!" He knocked Kade to the ground.

Daylor stepped in between Kade and Tanyl. "Stop it. Tanyl, you know you can't kill him. Just stop it. This is helping no one." He helped Kade up. "What will you do to help us? Please Kade, give us something."

Should he? The answer we so obvious. How was it that Tanyl couldn't see it? "Your prophecy holds the answer," Kade said. "After he gets the gnomes, who is there left to ally with?"

"No one," Daylor said.

Tanyl blinked. "You mean."

Kade nodded. "Yes, you won't have to find my nephew, Tanyl. Once he has the forces needed, he'll attack." He smiled. "He's done his father proud already."

"He'll kill you, too," Tanyl said.

"I know, but I'll die knowing that I didn't betray my family again." Kade turned towards the door.

"Kade, wait—"

Kade whirled around. "No. You want to kill another Ravenward? Do it yourself." Kade slammed the door behind him as he stormed out into the hallway.

HOURS LATER, Daylor was pacing around his large, elaborate chamber. On the wall, next to the window, was a small bookcase with a candle on top. It was filled with the spell books he'd collected during his long life. Ornate tapestries hung from the walls and a table big enough for four people was in the center of the room. On the far wall was his over-sized and unmade bed.

Circumstances have changed, Daylor thought. *I must see him.* If he was going to see Nyna, he must do so . . . privately. No one must know that he'd left the castle. But, how? He smiled. Bexon's Dimensional Tunnel, of course.

Daylor moved over to his bed and pulled a small chest from underneath it. *Please, Methos, let me have one.* He rummaged through his collection of spell components until he pulled out two rough diamonds. Enough for a two-way trip. *How much time will I have?* he wondered as he moved towards the door. *Not long.* Daylor slid the deadbolt on the door, ensuring himself some privacy.

He placed one diamond in a small pouch on his belt and put the other in the palms of his hands. "Dit onska ni jeg." His eyes were fixed on the glowing, rough diamond. "Dit onska ni jeg." A small light appeared on the wall before him, but his eyes never left the spell component. "Dit onska ni jeg." The light flashed. A magical archway where only darkness meets the eye appeared. Using the

Dimensional Tunnel was almost like an act of faith; the user never truly knows what's on the other side. Daylor closed his eyes and stepped inside.

He emerged from the tunnel into a small office in the tower of the Shadow Mage, one week's walk south of Staerdale Castle. The walls were lined with overflowing bookcases, and a mahogany desk was in the middle of the room.

"You could've knocked," Nyna said. Her white hair and light skin glistened in the candlelight. She wore a flowing red robe with silver fringe. Nyna took a sip of her hot tea.

Daylor grinned. "No, I couldn't, and you know it." He pointed at the chair across from her desk. "May I?"

Nyna leaned back into her chair. "Of course." She raised an eyebrow. "Trouble?"

"An opportunity," Daylor said. "Believe it or not, Kade is trying to find a way to betray Tanyl. He wants to save Galin."

"Oh, please."

"No, really. He feels . . . guilty about killing his brother." Daylor leaned forward. "Nyna, I really believe him."

She rubbed her chin. "Well, if it is true, having

two allies on the inside would certainly help when we attack the castle."

"Any luck with the Shadow Mage?"

Nyna frowned. "No. But, I did get a concession. He will let us use some of his apprentices, but only if they volunteer. He will not take sides in—how did he put it?—trivial matters."

Daylor laughed. "Trivial? That doesn't surprise me. He's probably a coward at heart, anyway."

"Maybe."

"I want to give Kade a chance to redeem himself. He has become a friend."

Nyna stared at him. "A Dark Elf with a heart? What will the gods think?" She smiled. "Sure, why not."

"Good. Do you have any volunteers?"

Nyna sipped her tea. "One hundred or so, for now. When the time is right, we'll be a tremendous asset to Galin's army." She gave Daylor a wry smile. "Even you would be useful."

He laughed. "Of course. What's the plan?"

"Brock, Galin's adoptive father, already contacted me. I'll meet him with my volunteers in Tarc."

Daylor leaned forward. "What do you want me to do?"

"We need intelligence. Troop levels, supply locations, military plans, etc. If Kade betrays Tanyl that could only help us."

Daylor nodded. "I think so too. I have to get back before someone notices that I'm missing."

"Glad you came in person this time. It's been too long," Nyna said as she stood up and shook his hand.

"Let's win this." Daylor cast another Bexon's Dimensional Tunnel and returned to the castle.

CHAPTER 8

"Up there! Look!" Ellis shouted as he pointed to the dragon flying overhead. "There it is again!"

Galin smiled as he looked upon the beast. "It's beautiful," he said as they rode northeast along the dirt road.

Mae laughed. "It's an animal."

Jena smiled at Galin. "You like it a lot, don't you?"

How well she knows me. "Yes. My magic is dragon magic, and a dragon could truly show me how to use my abilities . . . without hurting myself." He glanced towards the castle appearing over the horizon. "That must be it. Croglang Castle."

"Let's get it over with," Jena said as she galloped ahead.

Ellis laughed. "She's right." He cracked the reins and Runt charged after her.

Mae followed Ellis.

Galin watched his three friends ride towards the gnome castle. "I can do it." He followed them on the road heading for the castle.

As Galin approached Croglang Castle, his mouth dropped in its uniqueness. The walls were not stone, but iron. Strange balls of glass glowed, as if emitting some light. The great doors slid sideways along the castle walls rather than inward or outward. Two gnomes were standing outside of the gate wearing leather armor, carrying short swords. They were not checking visitors entering the castle. The gnomes simply looked upon Galin's party as they rode past them.

Ellis's eyes lit up as a flying toy flew near Runt's head. "Look at all this stuff!"

Inside the walls was more fascinating to Galin than the outside. Like other cities, the cobblestone roads lined the town within the walls like veins through a body. Vendors lined the streets selling their wares, but their goods were . . . like nothing Galin had ever seen before. There were flying things and long sticks that made a loud bang as they shot a projectile into a target. "What is all this stuff? This is incredible!"

Mae nodded. "Tanyl would want to know about this."

"Excuse me?" Jena asked.

Mae cleared her throat. "Nothing."

Jena frowned.

They continued down the main road towards the castle. The closer they got, the more excited Galin got. "Come on." He led them to the entrance.

Row upon row of hitching posts lined the outside of the castle, as if preparing for some kind of . . . conference. Galin tied Thea off. "Mae, would you stay and watch the horses?"

Mae nodded. "Sure."

Ellis smiled at Mae. "I'll stay, too."

"Fine." Galin looked into Jena's eyes. "Let's finish this." He and Jena headed towards the gate.

As they approached the castle entrance, three male gnomes wearing leather armor stopped them. "What's your business here?" the smallest one asked.

Galin tried to hide his grin, but failed miserably. "I'm Galin V of Ravenward, and I seek an audience with your king."

The gnome laughed. "Is *he* expecting you?"

"Umm, no. I don't think so."

All three gnomes burst out laughing. "Good thing, since we have a queen, not a king."

Jena bent down, eying the gnome. "Can we see your queen? It's about ridding our lands of the Darkstriders once and for all."

"One moment." The gnome disappeared inside.

Galin stared at her. "How'd you do that?"

Jena shrugged. "Some things just need a woman's touch."

"I guess," Galin said. He looked at the sun overhead. What would happen if they couldn't see her? Well, the alliance with the gnomes would be out, for one. If it failed, would they be able to kick the Dark Elves and their Darkstriders off the continent? Yeah, sure they could. He recalled when his adoptive father, Brock Feran, suggested using the gnomish flying machines to go over the walls. Almost immediately, visions of an army flying over the defenses and sliding down ropes draped over sides came to him. Once they hit the ground, his forces would fight towards the gate to let the rest of his army inside. Galin smiled. It would have been a great—

"Come on. Follow me," the gnome said as he reappeared from inside.

Jena smacked Galin in the shoulder. "You need to

stop daydreaming." She smiled as she followed the gnome into the castle.

The corridor walls were polished steel with iron grates for a floor. Tapestries that stretched from the ceiling to the floor sporadically hung on the walls. After navigating a few turns, they entered into the throne room. Six white columns were spread out with benches in between. On a raised dais were two thrones made of polished steel. There was a small table between them with an unidentifiable contraption on top with a mug sitting next to it.

A woman gnome sat on the throne. She had reddish-gray hair with green eyes. Her flowing purple robes were accessorized with a gem-filled golden crown and emerald earrings. She leaned forward as Galin and Jena approached. "Is it really you? How is it that you're alive?"

"My stepfather and stepmother saved me when Staerdale Castle fell," Galin said. "I'm told that Thea the Loyal—"

She leaned back in the throne. "Thea the Loyal. I remember hearing about her. She was like a sister to your father. My father negotiated a few trade deals with Axain when your father was on the throne."

Galin blinked. "I didn't know that."

"I'm sure there's a lot you don't know. Would you like some tea?"

"No thank you."

Queen Venfi looked at Jena. "How about you, my dear?"

Jena shook her head.

"Suit yourself." She pushed the mug underneath the contraption on the table and hit the red button. It began to whistle as the steam escaped through the top. In a moment, the tea poured out of the spigot just above the mug. When it was full, the machine shut down. Venfi took a sip. "Nothing beats the flavor of fresh tea."

"What is that?" Jena asked.

Venfi smiled. "Gnomish brilliance, child. A mixture of technology and magic. It is a machine that heats water without fuel and extracts the water from the moisture in the air."

"I love it," Galin said.

She put her mug down. "So, why are you here?"

Galin swallowed. "I seek an alliance with you. We're going to push the Darkstriders out of our homeland and we need your help."

"What kind of help?"

Galin grinned. "Some of your . . . gnomish brilliance."

Venfi picked up her mug and sipped her tea. "Like what?"

"Flying machines to fly over the defenses at Staerdale Castle, and some of those bang sticks."

Venfi frowned. "I figured as much. I'm sorry, but I can't help you."

"Why not?" Jena asked.

"First of all, the Darkstriders leave us alone because we don't get involved, and show everyone the *same* hospitality. Second, gnomes are a peaceful people. Most of us are not warriors or war mages or inventors, we're just simple people with the talent for creating machines embedded with magic," Venfi said. "We only fight as a last resort."

Jena stared right at Venfi. "What do you think will happen if we fail? Will they consider you blameless?"

"Probably not. But even if I wanted to, I couldn't," Venfi said.

"Why not?" Galin asked.

Venfi shifted in her seat. "We have an issue with a . . . a dragon. I know it sounds nuts, but it won't leave my people alone. They're constantly losing livestock to it."

"You want us to kill a dragon?" Jena asked. "You are nuts," she said under her breath.

"No, I don't want it killed. I just want it to move on, that's all."

Jena put her hands on her hips. "How the hell are we supposed to do that?"

Galin put his hand on her shoulder. "Hold on. If we do, will you join us?"

Venfi shook her head. "No, no way. Like I said, we are a peaceful people."

"We've got no reasons to help you then," Galin said.

"What do you want?"

Galin rubbed his chin. "Weapons. Flying ships with crews to fly them, and crowns to pay my army. Something like that."

Venfi smiled. "We make the best siege equipment on the continent and we sell it to everyone. But, you can have it for free, along with a few troops who know how to use it."

Galin frowned. "Not enough."

"Okay, fifteen flying ships."

He just stared at her.

"Twenty?"

"And?"

"Two hundred thousand crowns."

"We're talking about a dragon. Remember?"

Venfi's eyes sank. "Half a million crowns?"

"Done," Galin said as he shook her hand.

"Do you know where it is?" Jena asked.

Venfi nodded. "It lives in a sleeping volcano in the mountains to the east. About a day's walk."

Galin bowed. "See you in a few days then." He and Jena headed for the door. *How am I going to pull this off?*

WHAT AM I DOING? Kade asked himself as he looked at the portrait of his brother and his queen hanging in the Great Hall. He bit his lip. Kade wanted to right the wrongs he'd committed so long ago. Sure, he had been under Beldroth's spell, but was that really the reason? Or was it that his desire for power gave him the courage to do the only thing he could to become king? No, it wasn't courage. I was cowardliness.

His mind drifted back to when his brother married Nina. Kade had smiled with pride when the couple took to the dance floor. That was the night he'd met Beldroth for the first time. Her human beauty hid the Dark Elf lies. Only then did his jealousy become a wedge between him and Galin IV, not before.

Kade's and Galin IV's father taught them nothing

was more important than family. Every family eventually loses power and wealth, and all they would have was each other. On his father's deathbed, Kade promised to follow his teachings. Later, Kade tossed them aside when his sword skewered Galin IV. He gritted his teeth. Yeah, all because of that Dark Elf who made him believe that power was more important than anything or anyone. A lesson she taught by sacrificing her own life to save him. All that anger, that lust for power, and that hatred towards his nephew when he was just a baby, darkened Kade's heart to a point where there would be no redemption.

He looked around the room, ensuring that he was alone. A tear rolled down his left cheek. "Brother," Kade said to the painting, "like I've said thousands of times before, I'm sorry. I . . . I want you back, even if it means you're on the throne instead of me." He looked away. "This is crazy. I know you can't come back. But, I can help your son and put things right. I have shamed our father and betrayed our mother's memory. I was under Beldroth's control, but I can't say I wouldn't have eventually done something to take the throne from you. I am just a weak fool." Kade's eyes narrowed on Galin IV's face. "I will help your son take the throne and free our people. I'm not the warrior I was, but I have a greater weapon. I'm inside and . . . I'm not under suspicion. I'll kill Tanyl and help your son take the castle. I hope this will atone for my sins against our family." Kade moved closer to the painting. Tears flowed down both cheeks now. "Brother, forgive me. Please forgive me!" Kade sank to the floor, sobbing.

CHAPTER 9

Galin smiled as a refreshing mountain breeze beat back the heat from the sun. They had been riding for nearly a day. Sure, you could see the mountains from Croglang Castle, but their size made them appear closer than they were. The grasslands disappeared as they approach the base of the mountains. Tall pine trees lined the path into the mountains as if they were guarding it. He looked up. Just like the Wailing Mountains back home, these stretched beyond the horizon.

Ellis frowned. "How are we going to find it in this? They didn't actually give us directions."

"We go up. The volcano is supposed to be taller than the mountains," Mae said.

"What are we going to do when we find it?" Jena asked. "Shouldn't we figure that out first?"

Galin frowned. Yeah, Jena was right. What were they going to do when they found the dragon? Especially when the gnomes didn't want them to kill it. "Maybe, we talk to it."

"Are you nuts?" Ellis demanded. "We're talking about a dragon. They eat cows for a Saturday afternoon snack."

"Nyna said that I will need to talk to a master of dragon magic someday. Who better to talk to about dragon magic than a dragon?"

Ellis laughed. "Yeah, right. You can have a great chat as you're sliding down its throat. Tell you what; why don't you go and talk to it . . . alone. Of all the things we've faced, we never faced anything like a dragon before. Hell, we don't even have a clue how to fight it."

"We're not going to fight it. Let's follow the trail. Come on." Galin cracked Thea's reins and galloped up the mountain. He bit his lip. What were they going to do? Sure, he'd love talking to it, but it was an animal, not some person to be negotiated with. Just because it has natural magic doesn't mean it's intelligent or can even speak. Right? Maybe? Everyone has heard stories about dragons.

They were either savage animals or ancient beings with immense wisdom. Most likely, both are wrong.

"There's a clearing ahead," Jena said.

"I see it." Galin smiled at her. "Race you!"

Jena grinned as she urged Tyra forward, passing Galin.

By the time Thea was at a gallop, Jena was already in the clearing. She tied Tyra off onto a tree and pulled out the feedbag from the saddlebags. "I'm tired."

"We have been riding all day," Mae said. "The horses need to rest, especially after climbing the mountain."

"I was hoping to get to find the cave today," Galin started.

"Come on, Galin, relax a little," Ellis said as he jumped off Runt. "Besides, I'm hungry."

Mae laughed. "You're always hungry."

Ellis pulled an apple from his saddlebags. "Of course, I'm a man."

Was he right? Maybe. Galin's stomach had been grumbling, too. Sometime, Ellis made sense, even when he didn't mean to. "Okay, let's set up camp."

"I'll cook dinner," Ellis said. He pulled out a small sack of foodstuffs.

Mae was already gathering wood for the fire. "I'll help."

"Jena, come with me?" Galin asked.

"Where?"

He pointed to a bare rock above the trees, about twenty yards up the mountain. "Maybe we can see it from there. You know, just so we know where we're going in the morning."

She took his hand. "Sure."

Galin looked at Ellis and Mae. "We'll be right back."

"Where are you going?" Ellis asked. "Dinner will be ready in half an hour."

Mae slapped him in the back of the head.

"Ouch!" Ellis rubbed his head. "Why'd you do that?"

"They want to be alone, stupid."

Galin grinned. "It must be true love."

Jena tugged on his hand. "Leave them alone."

"Sure." Galin led Jena up to the rock overlooking the mountain range. The crystal clear sky enabled them to see for miles and miles.

"There!" Jena pointed straight ahead.

"Not what I expected," Galin said. Instead of rising above the mountains, the volcano was a little . . . shorter. "You really think that's it?"

Jena shrugged her shoulders. "Do you see another one?"

Galin pulled her in and kissed her. "No. What do you think? Half a day's ride?"

"I think so."

He hugged her. "I love you."

"I love you, too."

"Are you guys going to eat or what? I'm waiting for you!" Ellis yelled from campsite.

"Hungry?" Galin asked.

Jena grinned. "Men."

Galin led her back down to the camp. He smiled as the pleasant aroma from the pot over the fire hit his nose. "He could always cook."

"Better than me?" Jena asked with a grin.

"No, of course not," Galin said as he plopped down next to the fire. His stomach called out for Ellis's stew.

Ellis filled a small wooden bowl and passed it over to Galin.

"What's in it?" Galin asked.

"Don't ask," Mae said.

Jena took her bowl from Ellis. "Thank you."

Ellis dipped a piece of bread into his stew. "Did you see it?"

Galin nodded. "Yeah, it's about a half-day's ride from here, maybe closer."

Mae put down her spoon. "What do we do when we find the dragon?"

"I want to talk to it," Galin said as he leaned back against his pack. "Nyna once told me that dragons are ancient creatures with immense magical powers. Their power is within them. Magic to them is breathing to us. If Nyna is right, the dragon should be able to be negotiated with."

"If not?" Jena asked.

"Then we kill it."

Ellis frowned. "Are you nuts? A stupid ogre makes more sense than you. You're going to talk to an animal? Think about what you just said. Just because the gnomes are pacifists doesn't mean that—"

"Knock it off," Jena said.

The gem in Mae's ring had a slight glow. As she touched it, it glowed a little brighter. "Ellis, she's right. Can we change the subject?"

"Fine. I'm sorry," Ellis said as he plopped his spoon back into his bowl.

Mae smiled. "Ellis and I were talking about what we're going to do after we take back the kingdom."

Jena leaned in. "Do tell."

"If I can still stand the smell of him—"

"Hey!" Ellis protested. "I don't smell . . . that bad."

"I'd like to stay with him."

Galin swallowed. "What?"

Ellis's face went blank. "Are you asking me something?"

Mae looked away.

"That's my job."

Jena giggled.

"I am asking," Mae said as she gazed into his eyes.

Ellis kissed her. "Yes."

Mae put her bowl down and stood up. "Let's celebrate."

Ellis jumped to his feet and followed her like a puppy.

"That was . . . surprising," Galin said.

Jena embraced his arm. "Do you remember when you asked me?"

"Yeah."

"Hopefully, they actually *do* it faster than we did."

Galin hugged Jena. Was that a slight? It was true that Galin delayed actually tying the knot. At the time he said it was for her protection and his. But, was it? No, not at all. Galin knew he had second thoughts. His mind was made up when he nearly lost her. Yeah, hopefully they won't wait like he did. He smiled. "Knowing Ellis, they'll probably be married next week."

She embraced him. "Do you think you really can talk to a dragon?"

Galin's stomach dropped to his feet. "Sure, nothing to worry about." *Who am I kidding?*

THE RIDE to the base of the volcano was shorter than Galin thought the day before. As they ascended, the trees became shorter and more sparse. Rock intermixed with black soil covered the side of the volcano. "Look! What is that?" Near the top of the volcano appeared to be some kind of cave.

Ellis shrugged. "Maybe."

"I don't see anything else. Let's check it out," Jena said as she pushed ahead of Galin.

Galin grinned. "I'm coming. We need to stay together." He cracked Thea's reins and rode next to Jena and Tyra.

"You're so predictable." Jena tried to hide her smile.

"I am."

In the area immediately surrounding the cave, there were no trees or shrubs or even a weed, only a large mass of sharp volcanic rock. Galin looked down and swallowed. He pulled Thea's reins, stopping the mare from going any further. On the ground in front of them were piles of bones tossed about like toothpicks. But, these were bigger than toothpicks.

"What were they?" Jena asked.

Galin hopped down from his horse. Cows? Horses? They were livestock of some kind . . . had to be. "The Gnomes did say that the dragon was eating their animals."

Ellis grinned as he held up a small skull. "Looks like Gnomes, too."

Jena gasped. "Galin, I have a bad feeling about this."

"I know. I'm beginning to question it myself," Galin said.

"You've got your powers," Mae said. "I know you can kill it."

Galin frowned. "It is a dragon, and has dragon magic. I'm just a . . . novice. Besides, I don't know if it will even work on it."

Ellis grabbed Runt's reins and walked towards the cave. "The one thing I do know is, we're better off inside the cave than waiting for it to swoop us up."

"He's right," Mae said. "We can fight it better if it can't fly." She followed Ellis into the cave.

"I think we should go," Jena said.

Galin bit his lip. Something was wrong, he could feel it. Was it the dragon or something else? "Let's see what's in the cave." He grabbed Thea's halter and proceeded into the cave. His eyes widened the moment he stepped through the hole. The enormous chamber extended beyond the darkness. Soft dirt covered the cavern floor.

"This is awesome," Ellis said.

Mae pointed to a large impression in the dirt near the far wall. "That must be where it sleeps."

Galin swallowed. "It must be bigger than I thought."

Jena looked around. "Where is it?"

"Hunting for food?" Galin suggested.

Ellis's face turned a ghostly white. "I hope it's full."

"What do we do?" Mae asked.

What indeed? The dragon could return in a few minutes or a few months, Galin thought. How important were the flying ships to retaking the castle? If they had to actually breach the walls, the Darkstriders would be able to send for reinforcements and outflank them. They didn't have the time for a true siege of Staerdale Castle. No, they had to risk it or . . . give up on being king. "We wait. Back there in the shadows."

"How long?" Ellis demanded.

"Until it comes back." Galin looked towards the mouth of the cave. How long could they really afford to wait? Was he making a mistake?

A roar ripped Galin from his sleep. His heart raced as he jumped to his feet. His eyes never left the entrance. Nothing—well, nothing yet. Between heartbeats he looked around. Ellis and Mae were gone, only the blankets they slept under remained. Jena! Jena was gone, too. "Jena!" Galin yelled.

A shadow fell over the cave entrance. A sickening laughter, as if from a demon, echoed throughout the cavern.

Three skulls rolled from the entrance to Galin's feet. He knelt down. They were covered with spittle. Something spit them out! Were these his wife and best friends? He fell to the ground. They were dead, and it was his fault. Tears flowed down his cheeks as he curled up into a ball. He hugged one of the skulls. "Jena, I'm so sorry."

The laughter got louder.

Galin looked up.

It was enormous, bigger than the warehouse in Nia. The beast had red scales and wings like a bat. Its lizard-like head grinned at him.

He snatched his sword from under the blanket. Galin stared at the skull and the tingle from his heart turned into a burning. The tiny lightning arcs jumped across his skin. As they engulfed his sword it began to glow. "For Jena!" He charged at the dragon.

It reeled its head back like it was taking a breath.

Galin raised his sword over its foot. He looked up. Fire raced out of the dragon's mouth. Pain shot through his body. He'd felt nothing like it before. His sword fell to the ground as his arm incinerated. "Jena!" His world went dark.

GALIN JUMPED UP. Sweat was pouring off him. He looked around and saw Jena, Ellis, and Mae. He smiled. "I dreamed that—"

Jena's face had turned white. Her mouth opened but no sound came out.

"What is it?" Galin asked.

Without saying a word, Ellis pointed behind Galin. "It's back."

Galin swallowed. This was no dream. Slowly, he turned around.

It was huge, at least thirty yards long. The shiny scales were a deep blue and its wings were tucked along its sides. It sniffed them. "Humans?" The dragon smiled. "I haven't had a human in a long time. This will be a treat."

Ellis and Mae backed up against the wall.

Galin felt Jena at his side. Everything told him to run, but he couldn't. He had to do it. Galin wouldn't let his nightmare come true. No, not Jena. His will eroded with every step towards the dragon. "You can speak."

"Of course I can speak," the dragon said. "Your primitive tongue could be spoken by a hatchling. Before I sample you, I'm curious. Why are you in my home?"

Galin swallowed. "We're waiting for you."

It raised an eyebrow. "You want to die that badly?"

He shook his head. "No, that's not why we came. We . . . we want your help."

"Really?" it hissed. "You sound like one of those gnomes. They always start out like that, then I eat them."

His heart raced. Was this a mistake? "We're not gnomes."

It frowned. "I know that."

"Yes, they sent us, but that is not why we wanted to see you." He willed images of his mother slain by the Dark Elves to the forefront of his mind. A small tingle spread throughout his body until it turned into small electrical arcs jumping along his skin. Galin's eyes began to glow. "I need your help with my dragon magic."

It smiled. "Interesting." The dragon moved closer. "I've roamed the world for more than three thousand years and I've never seen this. This must be the work of the gods themselves."

Galin stepped back. "Will you help me?"

It backed away. "Maybe. What do you offer in return?"

He hadn't thought of that.

"What are you going to do with your power? Would you come back to claim your glory by killing me? Humans always attack me for their glory and I give it to them." It laughed. "Such a suicidal bunch."

"I have nothing to offer you. But, I need to learn so I can kill the Dark Elves that killed my family."

Its head jerked up. "Dark Elves? Did you say Dark Elves?"

"Yes," Galin said.

"The reason they are not in Fozzgart is because I keep them out."

"You protect the gnomes?" Jena asked.

It laughed. "No. I do it to keep them away from me."

"You know them?" Mae asked.

"Yes. You see, dragons mate for life, and we stay close to our hatchlings, even after they grow up. I am known among your kind as a blue dragon," it said.

"No kidding," Ellis said while trying to hide the shakiness in his voice.

Galin glared at him. "Shut up."

"My family lived in Setan. The Dark Elves hunted us down because their war mages use dragon's blood in their magic." Its eyes began to well up. "They killed them. They killed them all. I wasn't there." A tear rolled down its cheek.

"What did you do?" Galin asked.

"I killed them. Lots of them."

Mae frowned.

"One day, they cornered me and nearly killed me, too. That's when I came to Fozzgart. As long as they don't know I'm here, they'll leave me alone," it said. The dragon's eyes narrowed. "What do you intend to do?"

Galin smiled. "We're going to kick them out of Axain and send them back to Etrana."

"So you do have something to offer me," the dragon said.

Galin's face went blank.

"You offer me a victory to avenge my family."

"Will you teach me to use my dragon magic?" Galin asked.

"Better. I'm going with you."

"What's your name?" Jena asked.

It sat down across the cavern from Galin and the others. "You couldn't pronounce it."

"What should we call you?" Galin asked.

"Call me . . . Soreth. Yes, I'll be known as Soreth," the dragon said. "We'll start in a few hours." Soreth closed his eyes.

"Is he going to be your teacher or did he become our ally?" Mae asked Galin.

"Both, I think." *We can't lose,* Galin thought.

THE MOONLIGHT ILLUMINATED the cave entrance,

reflecting off Soreth's blue scales. He was looking down at Galin, like a master looks down at his pupil. "I've never had a human student before."

"I can do it," Galin said.

Soreth sighed. "I know you can, but that's not the problem."

"What is it?"

Soreth lowered his head, staring right into Galin's eyes. "You see, dragons, even young ones, don't have the single disadvantage that you do."

Galin pointed at his sleeping friends in the cave. "Everyone's depending on me. There's even a prophecy about me."

Soreth laughed. "Prophecy? Really? Do you really think that is why your friends follow you? Galin, you are naive."

Galin frowned. "I'm right."

"About a prophecy? Perhaps, but that is not why people follow you. I can see it in your eyes. You have courage, you're smart, and, most importantly, you care for others more than yourself." Soreth looked away. "I wouldn't be surprised if you really didn't want this life at all, rather it was forced upon you by circumstance."

Galin tore his eyes away. Images of finding Sarah, his adoptive mother, mutilated in her bedroom when he lived in Crey Village, appeared in his mind's eye. That was the turning point in his life and he knew it. "How do you know that?"

Soreth smiled. "Centuries of experience."

"I see."

Soreth stood up. "The disadvantage you have is that our magic destroys flesh. You may hurt yourself, not just your enemies."

Galin nodded. "I have to be careful. That's happened already. When I was in Tadus School of Magic, Nyna never let me forget that. She believed that it was my anger and rage that increased my power, but I had to control it so I wouldn't kill myself."

"That's nearly correct." Soreth leaned against the cave wall, staring out over the tree line below the volcano. "Get your sword and show me something."

Galin hurried back to the pack near the campfire. Grabbing his sword, he raced back to Soreth's side. With his sword in hand, he looked right into his eyes. "I'm ready."

"Proceed."

Galin willed images of Jena being captured by the Darkstriders. As his rage grew, a tingle from his heart spread throughout his body. Tiny lightning arcs began jumping across his skin. His eyes began to glow. When the arcs leaped from his hands to his sword, it began to glow. He felt the surging power run through his veins. He felt the familiar burning sensation on his forearms.

"Strange," Soreth said. "Your power is that of a youngling, but erratic." The dragon stared right into Galin's eyes. ~*Can you hear my thoughts?*~

Galin blinked. "What the—?"

~*You can hear me, can't you?*~

"Was that you?" Galin asked.

~*Yes, you know it is.*~ Soreth said without speaking. ~*Try it.*~

Galin closed his eyes. *Is this right?*

~*Yes.*~

How is this possible? Galin thought.

Soreth smiled. ~*All dragons can read thoughts. We don't use primitive tongues to communicate with each other. Our minds speak together, as if we are one. Can you feel it?*~

Feel what?

Soreth looked inside the cave, towards Jena, Ellis, and Mae. ~*The minds of your friends. You can hear their thoughts, too. All you have to do is try.*~

Should he? He would win every argument with Jena before they even happened. Galin could stop Ellis from blowing his relationship with Mae, before he did something stupid. After he won the throne, how powerful would he be at the negotiation table if he could read his opponents' thoughts? Galin would know their every feeling, every thought. He could get anything he wanted, while making them think it was their idea. Yes, such power, such—. Galin shook his head. "No, I can't do that. I would take away their privacy, their freedom to make their own choices. I will never do that. If I did it once, even for the best of reasons, I couldn't resist it for the wrong ones."

Soreth smiled. "Very wise. You aren't like most humans. I expected that you would be excited in the exploiting the thoughts of others for your own power. You surprise me, human."

"Was that a test?" Galin asked.

"No, but I liked your answer anyway," Soreth said. The dragon licked its lips. "There is one strange thing, well, besides a human using dragon magic. I'm not sure how you'll deal with the 'Transformation.'"

"What do you mean?"

"As young dragons mature, so do their powers, until it reaches the time for Transformation. At that time, the young dragon will hibernate for one hundred years and emerge a full-size dragon. I sense that you are near the time of Transformation."

Galin swallowed. "What will happen to me?"

Soreth laughed. "How should I know? You're not a dragon. Only by the gods will are you even able to use dragon magic."

"But, Nyna said some elves have used it before. The snow elves."

"Yes. A very few of them got great power from the Transformation. Others simply lost their powers, but most died."

"How?"

"Their bodies aren't designed to handle dragon magic and it consumes them. Imagine being burnt alive, and increase the pain a hundredfold," Soreth said. "It is not a blessing that you can use dragon magic, it is a curse. But, you are the only human I know that use it." He shrugged. "Who knows what will happen to you?"

Galin turned away. What did it all mean? Was the prophecy wrong? Was it all some sick joke by the gods? Did all those people who died to save him from the Darkstriders, since he was a baby, die for nothing? No, no way. Even if this was some twisted joke by Methos, he'd turn it around on the goddess. Yeah, he'd draw strength from it. If the *Transformation* turned him into a ball of fire, he'd take those bastards with him. He'd make Jena the Queen of Axain, just as he promised, even if it cost him his life.

He swallowed. Did she—would she—even care about that, once he was gone? Would she be so filled with grief that nothing else would matter? He shook his head. "How long do I have?"

Soreth frowned. "Again, you're human, not a dragon or even an elf."

"Tell me!"

"Three moon cycles, at the most. Not a lot of time, but enough for us to punish the Dark Elves." Soreth moved his mouth closer to Galin. "Remember, you promised me a chance to help you kill them."

Galin looked back at Jena. "Who will look after her?"

"Not my problem." Soreth spread his wings. "I'll be back in the morning with breakfast."

Galin watched the blue dragon fly high into the air. *Three months to live? What am I going to tell Jena?*

CHAPTER 11

The sunlight peered into the cave, prying Galin's eyes open. Jena, Ellis, and Mae were stuffing their packs, as if getting ready to leave.

"What's going on?" Galin asked while rubbing his eyes.

"Time's running out," Mae said.

A huge shadow fell over the cave. Galin whipped his head towards the entrance as the cow in Soreth's claws let out a terrified cry. The dragon tore the back leg off the cow and tossed it inside. "Here, have some breakfast. I'll have mine on the peak."

Galin stared at the bloody leg lying at his feet. "Thank you, I guess."

The dragon smiled. "Enjoy."

"Soreth, we're leaving," Galin said. "When will I

see you again?"

Soreth snapped the cow's neck, silencing the animal. "I will follow you." *~I'll always be near, trust me. I want revenge more than you do.~*

Galin stared right at the dragon. *What do I tell the gnomes? They'll only help us if you stop killing their livestock.*

~Tell them, I'll . . . cut back. If not, just make something up.~

"You got it," Galin said.

Ellis pulled out his daggers and rushed towards the cow leg. "Can't let this go to waste." He started slicing off pieces and tossing them into a sack.

Galin watched Soreth disappear. "May Odella protect us."

"Think he'll come back?" Jena asked.

He looked into her eyes. Should he tell her? What would he say? No. She'd worry herself to death and nothing more. No, he had to keep the Transformation to himself. If he was to die, it should be the best three months of his life. Why worry her? Galin smiled. "I think so. He said he'd help us."

Mae tossed the pack over her shoulder. "With a dragon on our side, we can't lose."

"Done," Ellis said as he tossed the small sack into his pack. "Let's go."

Galin nodded. "All right," he said as he grabbed his stuff and followed them out of the cave.

GALIN'S BUTT hurt from the day's ride. He smiled at Jena as Croglang Castle came into view. He longed to be alone with Jena. The sun began to set as they entered the castle walls. Music and gnomish laughter from the local taverns spilled out onto the street.

"I'm up for a drink," Ellis said as his eyes wandered towards The Tipsy Dove Tavern and Inn.

Mae grinned at him. "I'll join you, if you like."

Ellis licked his lip. "I'll get us rooms, first. Then I'll buy you an ale."

"Sounds good," Mae said.

Galin felt Jena take his hand. Yeah, this was a good day for the cause. Whether or not the gnomes help may be irrelevant. What could they do with Soreth's help? Perhaps, the better question would be, what couldn't they do? He looked into her eyes and smiled. When the Transformation hits, it might destroy her, right? Perhaps it is better that they don't have a child. When the father possess dragon magic, would it pass along to the son? Galin didn't realize his potential until puberty, but it doesn't mean an infant couldn't have powers, too. The dragon magic nearly killed him many times and he knows how to control it. What happens to a baby in the womb if it does have dragon magic? His throat went dry. What would happen to the mother? His mind went round in circles as he became lost in her—

Jena snapped her fingers. "Hey, you in there?"

Galin blinked. "Yeah. Sorry."

"I got the keys," Ellis said. He handed a room key to Galin. "Here you go."

Mae smiled. "Where's ours?"

"Right here," Ellis said as he dangled it in front of her face.

Mae grabbed his hand. "Let's get a drink."

"See you in the morning," Ellis said as he followed Mae to the bar.

"Think they'll get married?" Jena asked.

Galin grinned. "Ellis wants something tonight all right, but it's not marriage."

"Men! You're all the same." Her magnetic eyes caught his. "Let's go to our room."

Her coy look meant only one thing and Galin knew it. A few days ago, he'd jump at the chance to make love to his wife, but not now. He let on a tiny smile. "I'm ready to go to bed. I'm too tired." *I can't believe I'm saying this!*

She pulled him towards their room. "We haven't christened this inn yet. You can sleep after."

Jena and Galin navigated through the crowd towards the stairs in the back. His head was screaming no, but his body was screaming yes. Would she be upset if he said no? Headache? Should he just tell her? No, no way.

The stairs led to a simple hallway with eight doors. Jena slipped the key into room number three. "Here we are."

Galin swallowed as he followed her into the room. They'd made love tons of times since they were married and she never got pregnant. It must be hard to get pregnant, right? Yeah, what are the chances? Slim to none? Was that Galin's head or his hormones talking himself into making love with Jena? What's the worst that could happen? Galin drew her in and passionately kissed her. He smiled as he closed the door. *This is going to be a good night.*

ELLIS SAT NEXT to Mae at a round table in the corner with unusually tall stools. He smiled at Mae as he got consumed by her eyes. "I'm glad we ran into you in Nia. I've never met anyone like you before."

Mae beamed at him. "Are you saying that because you mean it or because you want something?"

"I mean it. I—never mind."

"What?"

Ellis blushed.

"Want an ale?" Mae asked.

"Sure."

Mae rose to her feet. "I'll be right back. You're buying the next round."

Ellis frowned. "You could just ask the bar wench."

"Yeah, but I don't want to wait. Be right back."

Ellis watched her move across the floor like a majestic swan swimming along the surface of the water. He licked his lips. Thoughts and desires raced through his mind. Yes, finally, they would be together. She'd been promising for months, but tonight it would finally happen.

Mae sat down next to another human at the bar amongst the sea of gnomes.

What is she doing? Ellis thought. A tease? Was she betraying him? He stared at her intently conversing with the man. It was almost like she knew him.

Mae stood up as she took the two ales from the bartender.

Ellis watched her walk towards the table. "Who was that?"

Mae sat down and slid an ale across the table. "An old friend. Someone I knew from Nia."

"Here?"

Mae sipped her ale. "Yeah, I was surprised, too."

"Is he going to join us?" Ellis asked.

Mae shook her head. "No. I told him we were having a special night."

Ellis shifted in his seat. Why would she not invite him over for at least one drink or to introduce Ellis to him? He smiled. "I'd like to meet him."

The blood drained from Mae's face. "No, you can't."

"Why not?"

"Because . . . you can't." She started to rub her ring. It began to glow.

Fog rolled into Ellis's mind. *What did I ask her?*

Mae's thin lips twisted. Her eyes intently gazed into his. "You didn't see anyone."

Ellis's face went blank. "See who?"

Mae kissed him. "Let's finish our ales and go upstairs. I want to see if what I heard about having sex with you humans is true."

Ellis's heart raced. His throat became dry. "Great." He blinked. *Why did she say 'you humans'?* He shrugged. After all, he was going to have sex.

CHAPTER 12

Galin's stomach began to rumble as they walked through the corridors in Croglang Castle the next morning. With Jena by his side, still glowing from last night, they came to a pair of elaborate metal doors with ornate markings. There were two gnome guards just outside the door.

"You'd think they weren't expecting us," Ellis said.

Mae grinned. "Maybe they thought you wouldn't make it back."

Ellis kissed her. "You mean we, right?"

Galin rolled his eyes. "Please stop."

Ellis laughed. "Now you know how I felt."

Jena elbowed Galin in the ribs.

"Queen Venti is expecting us," Galin said to the

guards.

"Who are you?" one of them asked.

"Prince Galin V of Ravenward. I've returned from the quest she sent us on."

"One moment." The guard slipped inside, closing the door behind him.

Ellis patted the other gnome on the head. "Do you fellas ever get taller than waist-high?"

The gnome glared at him, but said nothing.

"Well?" Mae giggled.

Galin smacked Ellis's hand away. "Knock it off. We need their help, *remember*?"

"Yeah, but not his," Ellis said.

The double doors swung open, revealing the throne room. There were many tapestries of gnomish achievements hung on the polished steel walls. The six white columns lined the path leading to the two steel thrones. Unlike before, the small table was missing.

Queen Venfi shifted in the throne. "I'd about given up on you. Everyone we sent before never came back."

That's because none of them possessed dragon magic. "I'm sure it was just my good fortune," Galin said.

"Did you even find the dragon?"

"We did and I . . . talked to it."

The queen blinked. "You what?" Her gaze narrowed. "How? I asked you to stop it from feeding on our livestock and you come back telling me that you talked to it?"

"It does speak," Ellis said. "Didn't the others tell you that?"

Queen Venfi frowned.

"Oh yeah," Ellis said, "they're all dead. Maybe they were in that pile of bones we saw just outside its cave."

"My cousin was one of those brave souls."

Galin glared at Ellis. "Shut up or get out."

"But—"

Galin raised his hand, silencing Ellis. "I'll do the talking. Understand?"

Ellis bit his lip.

"Please ignore my friend, he's tired from our . . . encounter with the dragon," Galin said.

"Were you successful?"

"Yes. As I was saying, we spoke to the dragon. He swore—"

"He? Not it?"

"Yes, he. He is an ancient creature that comes from Setan and was driven out by the Dark Elves. He said he will cut back on eating your cattle, but he needs a little," Galin said.

"So, you failed," Queen Venfi said.

"Can you blame a wolf from hunting sheep? Could you survive if you weren't able to eat?" Galin pointed at her plump waist. "And that happened when the dragon was not cutting back on your cattle."

Jena's jaw dropped. "Galin!"

"If you ask me, the castle could cut back some and you'd be more healthy because of it."

Queen Venfi's face turned blood red.

Did he make a mistake? Why was he being such a jerk? This was not him. It was almost as if someone was—he looked directly at Mae's finger. Her ring was glowing, again. He closed his eyes, forcing those thoughts from his mind. It was too late to change tactics. "Your Majesty, he will cut back. He will only eat them if, and only if, he can't find wild game."

"You called me fat." She tapped her rolls. "I'm not fat!" With her face redder than ever, she leaned forward.

Galin swallowed. He blew it. They'd be lucky to get hung. He killed his wife and his best friend. *What have I done?*

"I'm not fat. I'm huge." Queen Venfi rolled back in her throne, laughing. "You're certainly brave . . . or very stupid. I've never had anyone state the obvious facts before." She waved at the gnomes in robes behind her. "My advisers would never say that to me. Instead, they whisper it in secret in the corridors."

What the hell just happened? Galin thought.

"Your honesty and frankness will be a welcome breath of fresh air to the stuffiness of royal negotiations. You will make a great king," Queen Venfi said.

"Thank you, Your Majesty."

"I'll give you ten airships and the crews to fly them, on one condition."

"What condition?" Galin asked.

Queen Venfi smiled. "As soon as you retake your kingdom, we are invited to the king's court in Staerdale Castle. The gnomes have never been welcome before. We shouldn't be segregated simply because we act and look a little different. Our society has much to offer the people of Axain, after the Darkstriders are sent across the Fadyhl Waters."

Galin smiled. "Very well." He extended his hand to Queen Venfi. "Please accept my hand in friendship."

She shook his hand. "You will be a great king."

"Thank you," Galin replied. *We did it!*

Two hours later, Galin, Jena, Ellis, and Mae arrived with their mounts at the Air Dock, just north of Corglang Castle. The airships were tied off onto platforms high above the ground. There were strange discs that rose from the ground, bringing the party to the platform. The airship attached to the platform was five times as long as it was tall. On the rear of the vessel and along the sides were large cylinders with a red glow emanating from the end away from the ship. The deck was enormous, big enough for at least fifty soldiers. Towards the rear of the deck was a two-story structure with the ship's wheel on top, over-looking the deck.

A flamboyant gnome with glasses and a short sword by her side bowed in front of Galin. "Your Majesty, may I present the flagship *Reliant*."

Galin smiled. It was magnificent. "What's your name?"

"Captain Tanris Stormgear at your service." He motioned them towards the ship. "Please come aboard."

A grin stretched across Ellis's face. "This is great."

"Thank you, Captain," Jena said.

"Let's do this." Galin and the others boarded the *Reliant*.

Ellis looked over the side. "Are you sure about this? I don't have wings, you know."

Mae slapped him on the shoulder. "Shut up." She pushed Ellis onto the deck.

Gavin watched the gnome untie the mooring from the Air Dock. Yeah, Ellis was right. The ship would be flying high in the sky. Much higher than the walls at Staerdale Castle.

"Where to?" Tanris asked Galin.

He smiled. "To Tarc. My father is waiting."

Tanris saluted Galin. "Aye, sir."

Gavin watched the captain rush around the deck barking orders at his crew. Brock will be so proud of him, not only allying with the Dwarves and the Gnomes, but a dragon, too. He looked towards the volcano where they'd found the blue dragon, Soreth. He closed his eyes, trying to extend his thoughts as far as he could. *Soreth, are you there?*

~I'm here, young human. I'm high above you. I hunger for Dark Elf flesh,~ Soreth said with his mind.

Gavin look up. All he saw were the clouds high above them. *I don't see you.*

~I'm in the clouds.~

Jena tugged at his arm. "What is it?"

"The dragon. He's following us to Tarc."

Jena looked up. "Where?"

"Close, real close." He kissed her forehead. "Let's get some rest. There will be no time once we arrive."

Jena hugged him. "I know."

Gavin and Jena went below deck.

AM I MAKING A MISTAKE? Kade thought as he walked down the corridor towards Daylor's chambers. Sure, Daylor hated the Darkstriders as much as he did, but asking him to betray his own people was different, especially since it would mean killing them. Worse yet, he had nothing to offer him. No crowns, titles, lands, nothing. Why would anyone help him when they had nothing to gain? Would he? No way in hell would Kade agree to this, so why should he expect Daylor to? Kade turned a corner.

"Good morning, Your Majesty," a passing Dark Elf knight said.

"Morning," Kade replied without even looking at him. Was that Dark Elf really that bad? He was just doing his duty, like his father had taught him and Galin IV when they were boys. His eyes began to well up. Why did he kill his twin brother? Power, the lust for power and Beldroth's influence. Kade already decided that he had to do somethings, but what? He stopped in front of a simple door and knocked.

"Enter," Daylor said from behind the door.

Kade pushed the door open, smiling at Daylor. "How are you this morning?"

Daylor was sitting behind an elaborately carved mahogany desk. An unlit candle sat on the corner, right next to a steaming cup of tea. His chambers were neat, with only three pieces of furniture and rows of overfull bookcases. He looked up. "Fine, just trying to get my morning reading done."

Kade motioned towards the bed. "May I?"

"Sure." Daylor leaned back in his chair. "You are being unusually polite. Do you need something?"

Kade bit his lip. Was he that obvious? "I have a question for you. Hypothetically, of course."

A smile stretched across Daylor's face. "I do like games. Ask away."

What do I do if he doesn't side with me? Kade thought. "Are you happy with Tanyl?"

"What do you mean?"

"Are you happy?"

"With what?"

"With . . . your station here," Kade said.

"Are you offering me something?"

Kade shook his head. "No, I have nothing to offer. Well, that's not true."

Taylor sighed. "What are you offering?"

"A chance at new life, if you want one," Kade said.

"Let's assume I do, hypothetically, of course."

"Of course."

"What do you want from me?" Daylor looked intently at Kade, as if trying to determine his true intentions.

"I have to save my nephew and my people from the Darkstriders . . . from Tanyl," Kade replied.

Daylor sipped his tea. "What's your plan?"

Plan? He hadn't got that far yet. Would Daylor lose interest if he thought that Kade hadn't really thought this through? Kade cleared his throat. "We know from the intelligence reports and our source that Galin already allied with the Dwarves, the Gnomes, and a dragon."

"Don't forget the Vulwin Elves," Daylor reminded him.

Kade nodded. "I didn't forget. My point is that they must be getting ready to make a run on the castle."

"Why would they risk a siege?" Daylor asked. "Tanyl would send for reinforcements and wipe them out."

"I know, that's why I believe whatever they're planning, it will be quick," Kade said.

Daylor sighed. "You still haven't told me what

you need from me."

"I need help killing Tanyl at the right time. The Darkstriders are a very top-down organization and when we kill him, there will be some confusion, to say the least."

"And the soldiers will be demoralized," Daylor said. "Brilliant."

"His body must be public for all his followers to see."

"What about Ruyl?" Daylor asked. "He rarely leaves Tanyl's side, when he's here."

"I don't know yet. But, we have to do one more thing."

Daylor leaned in. "Yes?"

"We have to get word to my nephew, so Tanyl's death is properly timed. If we do it too early, your king would just send another in Tanyl's place. He or she would clamp down on security so hard that we would just made things worse. If we do it too late, we lessen my nephew's chance for success." Kade looked away. "This is the only way I know to repent for the sins I committed against my family," Kade said.

"I understand why you're doing this, my friend," Daylor said. "But, I don't see why I should help you. You have nothing to offer me for my . . . assistance."

Kade shrugged. "I have no crowns, magic, lands, or titles to give you." He laughed. "I can't even guarantee that my nephew won't kill me on sight, let alone you. A Dark Elf." His face fell as he stood up. "I'll understand if you can't help me, but please keep this to yourself." Kade headed toward the door.

Daylor held up his hand. "Wait. I never said no." He motioned Kade back to the bed. "Please, sit."

Kade obeyed.

"I already know your nephew. In fact, I was at his graduation from the Tadus School of Magic."

Kade blinked. "How? You never leave the castle."

"Magic, of course. I can get a message to his mentor, Nyna."

"Who?"

"The snow elf that tried to train him in dragon magic." Daylor moved over towards Kade, putting his hand on Kade's shoulder. "You see, I'm already on their side. I assure you, Galin will not kill me. I'm not so sure about you."

Kade stood up. "Does this mean . . ."

Daylor nodded. "Yes, I'll help you."

"Thank you," Kade said as he shook Daylor's hand. "Thank you for helping my family." He left the room, closing the door behind him. *Are there others within the castle walls against Tanyl, too?*

CHAPTER 13

Gavin sat on the deck with his back to the cabin with Jena, Ellis, and Mae sitting around him. The hot midday sun beat on his already burnt neck.

"How are we going to do it?" Ellis asked.

"Do what?" Gavin asked.

"Take the castle. What else would I be talking about? Jeesh, for a prophesied king, you're pretty damn slow."

Mae smacked Ellis in the shoulder. "Take it easy. He'll be the king and have you flogged."

Jena giggled. "I'd love to see that."

"Maybe I'll just do it for fun." Galin grinned at his best friend, who didn't return in kind. He cleared his throat. "Anyway."

"Well? What's the plan?"

"Do we have to talk about it right now?" Gavin demanded.

Ellis frowned. "What else are we going to do? We've been on this flying coffin for nearly two days now."

Galin looked around. "Why not?" He leaned towards his friends, lowering his voice. "My father figures that a siege of Staerdale Castle would take at least a year, and the Darkstriders would send reinforcements or use magic to overwhelm us. First, we cut off any reinforcements at Port Eldham. He said the port used to be a fortress against any naval attack."

"But they lost it when the Darkstriders took over," Mae said.

Galin nodded. "Yeah, but they were already on the land, not coming from the sea."

"Oh."

"Once we have the port, then we attack the castle itself," Galin said. "We fly over the walls and let the rest of our forces inside. Simple."

Ellis laughed. "Yeah, right. Keep dreaming."

"Who would do that?" Mae whispered.

Gavin grinned. "I have someone in mind. He's the

best I know and a real pain in the ass." His eyes wandered towards Ellis.

He stopped laughing. "No way. I won't do it. You're asking me to kill myself."

Galin frowned. "I'll be with you. Besides I wasn't asking."

Ellis looked over at Jena. "Am I supposed to save his ass again?"

"No," Jena said. "I'll do that myself, again. I'm going, too. You're not scared, are you?"

Ellis's face turned red. "No. I—"

Galin started to laughed.

"I'm not afraid," Ellis said. "I'm just . . . smart."

"You won't come with us?" Gavin asked.

Ellis sighed. "Fine, I guess someone has to save the kingdom. Too bad you need me to do it."

Gavin hugged Jena. Everything was going better than he thought. No, things were perfect. What did he forget? Nothing. What could possibly go wrong?

Daylor strolled across his chambers and opened the door. He peered up and down the corridor. Nothing. To cast Bexon's Dimensional Tunnel was no quiet matter. He closed the door. What should he tell Nyna? Sure, Nyna was still at the Tadus School of Magic, but he should be packing up to join Brock and the prince. How many volunteers did they get? Did they even stand a chance against Tanyl's killers? No, not without magic and a little . . . treachery. Daylor pulled out two rough diamonds from his desk and stared at them. What if they failed? What would happen to him then? Tortured by the seers or fed to the Feral Orcs. What if they won? What would he gain? A hearty handshake and a job well done. Was that really worth the risk? Maybe, maybe not. Perhaps it was better to play both sides, for now. He tossed one of the diamonds into his pocket and held the other in the palm of both hands. "Did onska ni jet," Daylor said. The rough diamond began to glow. "Did onska ni jet." A light shot out from the diamond onto the wall, forming a dark hole in the air. "Did onska ni jet." The small hole jumped into an archway-like black hole. "Nyna, are you at home?" He stepped into the darkness and the portal slammed shut behind him.

"Why are you here?" Nyna demanded. "This is not neutral ground anymore."

The light hurt his eyes as he emerged from the dimensional tunnel. Daylor blinked. As his eyes began to clear, he looked around the room. He was in Nyna's bedchambers, as he'd anticipated. The walls were lined with overflowing bookcases and tables with piles upon piles of scrolls. The piece of furniture not littered by books or scrolls was her bed. It was a simple twin bed with a brown wool blanket. Nothing in her room showed her true wealth. "How can that be? Tadus School of Magic was always neutral ground."

Nyna tossed another robe into a sack. "Not anymore."

"What happened?"

Tears rolled down Nyna's face. "I did it."

Daylor cocked his head. "Why? What happened?"

Nyna ripped her eyes away from him. "I . . . I chose a side. Once word got out, Tanyl sent his pyromancers to destroy us." She sat down on the bed. "If I . . . if I just didn't get involved the school would go on."

"The school, is it all right?"

Nyna frowned. "No. But, we fought them off. All of us. Even the Dark Elf students."

"Tanyl will kill them and their families, calling them sympathizers."

"In the end, we killed or morphed just about all of them." Nyna wiped her eyes. "There was one Dark Elf who wasn't magical; he burst through the hole their mages put into the castle walls. He killed teachers, the headmaster, students—"

Daylor pulled her in close to him with a gentle hug. "It's over now."

She was crying on his chest. Her teary eyes looked up into his. "Daylor, he murdered little boys and girls. Human, Vulwin Elves, Gnomes, and, yes, even Dark Elves."

"I thought you won," Daylor said.

She nodded. "We did. The Shadow Mage and his army war mages came to our rescue and overwhelmed them. That Dark Elf got away. They called him Ryul."

Daylor jumped back. "Ryul? Surely, not."

Nyna nodded. "Yes. There's no mistake."

"How did they know to attack the school? How did they know you chose a side?"

"I don't know. Someone must have told them." Her cheeks were red. "Some even said it was you!"

"Well, it wasn't," Daylor said. "What about the rest of the students and faculty?"

"I closed the school down and sent everyone home." She stared right into his soul. "You still haven't answered my question, why are you here?"

Perhaps, I did choose the wrong side, Daylor thought. He smiled. "I bring you good news."

"I could use some."

"Kade wants to kill Tanyl."

Nyna waved him off. "Please. Even if he did, the price would be too high to be worth it."

Daylor nodded. "Normally, I'd agree with you, but things are . . . different."

"How so?"

"Guilt. A very powerful emotion in humans. He regrets—"

"What? Murdering his family for the throne?" Nyna laughed. "Only now he feels remorse? What a pig!"

Daylor sat down on her bed. "Regardless of the timing, he wants to change things."

"How?" Nyna demanded. "Galen's parents were noble rulers and wonderful people. Kade was always the dark sheep of the family, wanting power more than anything else. I bet his father gave thanks to Odella every night that Kade was born thirty seconds after Galin. Talk about a family disgrace."

Daylor glared at her. "Are you done?"

"I guess."

"He wants help killing Tanyl," Daylor said.

"Why does he need help?" Nyna asked. "Just walk into his bedchambers and slit his throat."

Daylor shook his head. "No, you can't do it like

that, if you want to survive it. I've got no idea how he wants to do it. Only that he wants my help in doing it."

"I trust you, Daylor, not him. Remember that."

"Kade doesn't think killing him would be the problem. It's more about the timing."

Nyna leaned forward. "Go on."

"If he does it too early, the Dark Elf king will just send a replacement with additional troops and pyromancers, which will stop any chance Galin has in taking back the kingdom. If he does it just prior to or during the attack, it—"

Nyna grinned. "It will confuse and disrupt the Darkstrider forces. Brilliant. Are you sure he came up with that all by himself?"

"I'm sure. He interrupted my studies to tell me about it."

"So, all he needs is to know when Galin is attacking the castle, right?" Nyna asked.

"Correct," Daylor replied.

Nyna nodded. "Okay. What if he's lying?"

"He's not."

"Humor me for a second. What if he is?"

Daylor swallowed. "He'd warn the Darkstriders and they would destroy Galin's forces easier than they did the school."

"And Kade would be the hero of the Darkstriders for their king across the Fadyhl Waters," Nyna said. "He'd take Tanyl's place in ruling over Axain. Someone with Kade's ambition, he'd try to conquer the rest of the continent with the king's blessing."

Was she right? Was Kade playing Daylor for a fool? Perhaps, perhaps not. It was no secret that Kade was ruthless and took out anyone in his way. Even him? Maybe. True, it was completely out of character for Kade to be . . . regretful. If he was Kade, what would he do? Yeah, no question. Power is too tempting. Betting on a prophecy had been a sure thing, but was it still? A smart Dark Elf only bet their lives on sure things. *What should I do?* Daylor thought. "Kade recruited me."

The blood drained from the snow elf's face. "Does he know your involvement in the school?"

"No, but he knows I already switched sides," Daylor said as he stood up. *Was it too late to change back?*

"Do you trust him?"

Daylor nodded. "I think so. At least enough to give him enough rope to hang himself and no one else."

"Good idea." Her blue eyes blinked. "What will you tell him?"

"Are you going to meet them?"

"Yes."

"How much warning can you give me? I need to know soon, but I won't tell him until the attack is within 24 hours, okay? Just in case," Daylor said.

"I'll teleport a scroll onto your bed. That way we can keep our communication . . . private."

"Very well. I'll be expecting it." Daylor pulled the other rough diamond from his pocket. "I'll see you soon."

Nyna shook his hand. "May Odella's light shine on us both."

Daylor smiled. *Which side is more profitable for me? The prophecy is no longer a sure thing. Whom do I betray?* He cast Bexon's Dimensional Tunnel and the portal appeared right in front of Nyna's bedchamber door. "Good-bye. I'll see you again." He stepped through the portal.

Daylor opened his eyes as he emerged in his bedchambers. The light blurred his vision. After a few moments, he walked over to the mirror on the wall. Staring at himself, he frowned. *Whom do I betray?*

CHAPTER 14

Galin felt a small hand shake him.

"Sire, we're here," Tanris said.

"At Tarc?"

Tanris nodded. "Yeah, kind of."

"What do you mean?"

"I'm not landing in Tarc, just outside of it, far enough to keep the air ships out of sight."

"Good plan." Galin looked over at his friends, who were already stirring because of the morning sun prying their eyelids open. "Get up. It's time to go." He looked back at Tanris. "How long till we land?"

"About ten minutes," Tanris replied. "Your party will be on your way soon."

"I want you to come with us," Galin said.

"Why? I'm here to drive, not fight."

"True, but you command these ships, right?"

"Yes."

"I want you to be involved in the planning. No one else that will be there knows the capabilities of your vessels better than you."

A smile stretched across Tarnish's face. "Of course I'll come. I—" He bolted across the deck, barking orders at a deckhand.

Galin grinned. Everything was going great. This was going to be easy, right? After all, the prophecy said so.

"I'm ready," Jena said.

"Me, too," Ellis said.

"Let's finish this," Mae said.

"We're meeting my father at the Rusty Nail," Galin said.

"How will he know we've arrived?" Ellis asked. "It's not like you sent him a message or something."

"Starting with the new moon cycle, he was going to check the Rusty Nail every night. Not too complicated." Galin felt . . . lighter. He went over to the side. The ground was getting closer. They were landing. He pointed to a small town off in the distance. "That must be Tarc."

"It is," Tanris said.

"As soon as we land, we'll get the horses from below and meet Brock," Galin said.

Jena kissed him. "Soon, I'll truly be your queen."

He hugged her. "No matter what happens, you already are."

Ellis rolled his eyes. "You two make me want to throw up."

Mae elbowed him in the stomach.

"What did I say?" Ellis demanded.

Galin looked towards Tarc. *Can I finish it before the Transformation? How much time do I really have?*

After the *Reliant* landed, Galin, Jena, Ellis, and Mae mounted their horses and Tanris climbed on his pony. They started the short ride towards Tarc. The field that the air ships landed in were separated from Tarc by a thin strip of trees. Nothing strange about a farmer keeping a visual barrier between his or her livestock and the drunken locals and, in this case, very convenient.

As they emerged from the tree line, Tarc came into view. It was a quiet little town with no large buildings or, really, anything memorable. Perhaps that was why Brock wanted to meet here. Privacy. Nothing requires privacy more than plotting the overthrow of the Darkstriders.

About fifteen minutes later, Galin and the others

rode into town. The roads were not cobblestone, but dirt. The simple buildings he saw from a distance were once elaborate, but now unkempt. There were no merchants or children running about, just drunkards fighting in the street. "Not what I expected."

Ellis smiled. "My kind of place."

Tanris shook his head. "You humans are a bad lot. You've got no respect for yourselves."

Galin frowned. "This isn't our best side, that's for sure. Come on." He urged Thea forward towards the one-story building at the end of the street that was surrounded by passed-out drunkards. "Did they scare away the people?"

Jena frowned. "Galin, these people are in our army. This is our fault."

"You sure?"

"Yeah."

"Let's go inside," he said as he hopped down from Thea and tied her off onto the hitching post. *Where's my father?* he thought as he pushed his way inside.

Gavin's nose wrinkled as the aroma of day-old vomit smacked him in the face. There used to be twenty or so tables, but only one was still in one piece. The rest were busted up like firewood on the floor. The old man behind the bar was shaking whenever someone told him to give them an ale or whiskey. The place was unusually crowded for so early in the day.

A muscular man with brown and gray hair pulled back into a ponytail sat behind the only table still in one piece. Galin's heart lifted as he saw his adoptive father.

Jena ducked as a mug flew the through air, nearly hitting her in the face.

Rage. Who would dare nearly hit his queen? What pigs! The tingle flowed from his heart, spreading throughout his body. Tiny arcs, like lightning, began to bounce across his skin. Gavin's eyes began to glow. "Enough! The bar is closed. Everyone out."

"Whoooo thheeeee heelllll are yoouuu?" a soiled man asked.

Galin snarled at him. "Your king. Get out!"

As if they saw a demon, the drunkards fled.

Galin closed his eyes, willing the rage away, and his eyes returned to normal. He pulled up a chair across the table from Brock. "Father, are you all right?"

Brock was drinking coffee, not ale. "I am now. I'm glad to see you son."

Jena, Ellis, Mae, and Tanris sat next to Galin. "What happened here?" Jena asked.

"Well, at first the town welcomed us as heroes. Then, the soldiers got bored and started drinking. They drank so much, most of the town fled. I won't even tell you the crimes they did against these people. Not honorable at all." Brock looked over at the gnome. "Who's this?"

Tanris extended his hand. "Tanris Stormier, captain of the airship *Reliant*."

"He commands the airships that Queen Venfi gave us," Galin said. "And that's not all."

Brock leaned forward.

"Father, Soreth, the blue dragon, is helping us, too."

"What?" Tanris demanded.

"Really? Wow," Brock said. "That's very helpful."

"What about the others?"

"The dwarves and the Vulwin Elves arrived, Nyna, too, but—"

"But what?"

"Your school, Tadus School of Magic, was overrun by the Darkstriders."

Galin blinked. "How? That place was impregnable."

"Apparently not. The Shadow Mage was going to let some of the war mages help us, if they chose to, but that offer was rescinded."

"You mean no mages?" Galin asked. "Is that right?"

"Only Nyna," Brock said. "Perhaps the dragon will tip the balance in our favor. Anyway, we've got the headquarters and the rest of our forces in a cave system to the west." He stood up. "I'll take you there and we can finalize the plan."

Galin looked around. If this was what he brought to Axain then which is worse, the Darkstriders, or him? "No more of this. I mean it."

Brock nodded. "I'll recall everyone back to the cave to prep for the fight."

Galin followed his adoptive father out the door. *Can I still do this?*

BROCK LED Galin and the others out of Tarc towards the hills to the west. The fresh air invaded Galin's nostrils, bringing a smile to his face. "What happened? Why did you let our soldiers do that?"

Brock frowned. "Well, once we left Iron Fist Keep, they were on edge all the time. After we arrived, they let their hair down, but it got out of control. What can I say? I'm sorry."

"Father, it just makes it that much harder. How

can we promise the people a better life when our own soldiers trash their towns? Some folks can say one thing while trying to attain power and go back on their word once they achieved their goals. I won't do that," Galin said. "I'm sorry, but we can't let this happen again. Otherwise, Mother would have died for nothing. Is that what you want?"

Brock shook his head. "You know better than that."

Galin forced his eyes straight ahead. "Enough said. Is it far?"

Brock pointed to the tree line. "The cave entrance is just beyond those trees."

After they entered the woods, Galin hopped off Thea. "Let's stop for lunch. The horses need to be fed." He looked at Jena, whose face had become pale. "Are you all right?" he asked as he grabbed Tyra's reins.

"I'll be okay. Must be because I didn't eat break-fast," Jena replied as she climbed off her horse.

"You never eat breakfast," Ellis said. "Maybe you finally got sick of Galin," he said with a smile.

Mae glared at him. "And you wonder why I kicked you out before we made love the other night? Show the king some respect."

Ellis dismounted Runt and pulled out a sack of food from his saddlebags. "I'll start cooking."

"I'll build the fire," Brock said.

Galin touched Jena's cheek. "Are you sure you're okay?"

"I'm fine. I must be coming down with something." Jena sat down next to the fire pit that Brock was assembling.

"Okay." Galin joined her. He looked right into her eyes. *I'm so glad we don't have kids. At this rate, we may never have them.* The Transformation wasn't far off, and who knows what would happen. Hell, the dragon didn't even know. For all he knew, he was a practical joke by Methos, the goddess of the Shadows. The same deity the Dark Elves worship and fear. There was no certainty in their future or the kingdom. In the next thirty days, he'd probably be dead . . . or king. Galin bit his lip. He—

"What are you thinking?" Jena asked.

Should he tell her? "Nothing special." Galin smiled. "Feeling better?"

"A little. It'll pass," Jena said.

Ellis set up his stew pot over the fire. "We'll have lunch in about twenty minutes."

"Great," Mae said as she settled in next to Brock.

Galin stared at Jena. *Why is she sick?*

After an hour, they were on their way towards the cavern. The trees began to thin out, giving way to a small hill with a gaping hole in the center. Just outside the entrance were six creatures. Their skin colors ranged from green to gray. All were heavily muscled, with long hair and two teeth protruding from their lower lip. They were the Feral Orcs that had joined Galin at the Battle of Iron Fist Keep. Their leader, Yotul, was the only female Feral Orc among them. Her face was feminine and her chest was not dissimilar from a human female's.

"Welcome, Your Majesty," Yotul said. "Glad to see you made it."

"Thank you," Galin said. He looked at Brock. "This it? It doesn't look very big."

Brock and Yotul tried to hide their smiles.

Jena yawned. "Let's get inside, it's been a long trip."

"Come on," Brock said as he rode his horse inside the cave.

Galin felt a cool breeze with the stench of people coming from inside the dark cavern. The walls glistened in the torchlight from sconces sporadically placed along the corridor. He felt the gentle slope going deeper into the earth. The corridor was not more than a few yards wide, forcing them to ride single file.

"The headquarters is in the first chamber, just ahead," Brock said.

After a few yards, Galin turned left into the main chamber. It was enormous, and bustling with activity. Tents huddled around campfires. Soldiers of all races were sharpening weapons and polishing their armor. The ceiling was at least thirty feet high. He squinted, trying to see the far end of the cavern but he failed. "How big is it?"

"We fit the Vulwin Elves, the Dwarves, and our fighters with siege equipment in this chamber. About five thousand fighters."

Galin followed Brock inside the largest tent in the center of the cavern. There was a huge round table surrounded by simple chairs. A makeshift throne sat at the head of the table. "This ours?"

Brock nodded. "Sum and her father donated it, as well as the other equipment. We've spent months down here training. Sum really helped us improve our soldiers' fighting skills."

"But not their behavior," Mae commented.

Brock bit his lip. "No. Ellis and Mae's tents are next door."

"We're off," Ellis said.

"Wait a minute." Mae wrenched her arm from his grasp.

Ellis frowned.

"Mae, I'm tired," Jena said. "Can you give us some privacy?"

"Sure." Mae and Ellis hurried out of the tent.

"What's in there?" Jena asked, pointing at the large curtain-like divider on the other side of the throne.

"Your quarters," Brock said.

Jena yawned. "I'm going to turn in."

"Okay," Galin said as he watched her disappear behind the curtain. "Do you have a minute?"

"Sure, son," Brock said as he sat down at the table.

Galin slipped down into the throne. "Do we really have a chance? I mean, without the war mages."

Brock sighed. "A dragon helps, but the war mages would have been better. We may have five thousand, but they have at least twice that, with mages, and they're behind the castle walls."

"I'm sorry for what I said earlier. It wasn't my place."

"No, you did the right thing. I was wrong and I knew better. I just—I just began to think that I'd lost you. You were gone for months. You're all I have left. There is no one else. Whenever I look at you, you remind me of Sally. I know she is with Odella right now, waiting for me. But, I'm not ready to go just yet. I want to see you succeed and to make sure that all those people who sacrificed their lives for you to retake the throne didn't die for nothing," Brock said.

Galin nodded. "I love you, Father. I won't let you down."

"I know you won't." Brock smiled. "Now, go and sleep next to your wife. We've got a lot of people meeting with us tomorrow, including some old friends," he said as he rose from the table. "Good night, son."

Galin watch Brock leave the tent. He sighed. *Can I really pull this off?* Galin walked into the bedchamber and laid next to Jena, who was already sleeping. He ran his fingers through her hair. *I can't let her down. I won't.*

CHAPTER 15

Galin's stomach twisted. Was it hunger or anxiety? The initial planning meeting was to start after lunch, but he'd never done anything like this before. Would he blow it? No, he'd have help to make sure he didn't. But King Faeler, the exiled Vulwin Elf king, was going to be there. Was he supposed to act a certain way? Talk a certain way? What was being royalty supposed to look like, anyway? Galin sighed.

~Just be yourself,~ Soreth whispered into his mind.

Galin closed his eyes. *You're here?*

~Yes, I'm here, just as I said.~

How?

~Blue dragons can shapeshift into anything we want. I'm here in your camp.~

Will you come to this meeting?

~Will the others accept me, like you did?~

Galin swallowed. *I don't know. Will you try?*

~Very well, I'll be there shortly.~

How will I recognize you?

~I'll enter the tent as a small black dog and transform myself into a human in front of everyone. That way, there can be no doubt,~ Soreth thought.

I'll see you then. Galin looked over at the entrance of the tent; no one had arrived yet. He sighed.

Jena emerged from the back part of the tent. "Aren't you a little early?"

Galin nodded. "I am. But, I'm—"

"There's no reason to be nervous," she said.

"Soreth is here."

"The dragon? How?"

Galin shrugged. "Don't know. But, he is. He spoke to me through magic. I—"

A tall Vulwin Elf with long, golden hair entered the tent. There was a small dove tattooed on her neck. "Galin! Jena!"

Gavin's heart lifted as he hugged Sumia, daughter of King Faeler. "It's so good to see you."

Sumia recoiled. "Um, this won't do."

"What do you mean?" Jena asked.

"As royals, you need to be the last ones at any meeting. Come on, go in the back," Sumia said. "I'll get you when it's time."

"Wait a minute," Galin protested.

"Who knows more about being royalty, me or you?" Sumia asked.

"You," Galin replied.

"Then trust me. My father is a stickler for royal traditions, and you need his help."

"Fine," Galin said as he and Jena went behind the curtain into their sleeping area. He plopped down on their bed. "I feel like my mother just sent me to my room.

Jena giggled. "Not very kingly of you."

Galin frowned.

"Just give her a chance," Jena said. "Remember, she helped us before."

Galin nodded. "I know. It's just—"

"What?"

"I'm nervous. I mean, what do they expect from me? Can I even deliver what they want?"

Jena's eyes softened. "People follow you because of who you are, not because of some stupid title or ancient prophecy." She kissed his forehead. "Galin, they believe in you, just like I believe in you. Your problem is that you need to start believing in yourself."

She's right, Galin thought. How many times had Jena eased his fears? Galin couldn't count that high. Perhaps that was what marriage was all about. Not raising children or sex or something to brag about to your friends who aren't married, but supporting one another, even in the most dire of times. "I love you."

Her eyes glistened. "I know."

Sumia stuck her head through the curtain. "They're ready."

"Let's do this," Jena said as she rose from the bed.

"Who's following whom?" Galin asked with a smile.

"They're following us."

"I wouldn't have it any other way," Galin replied as he stepped through the curtain into the next room.

Standing around the table were the other leaders who would help him in his quest to expel the Darkstriders from Axain. Galin swallowed. What would a king do? Would a king just sit and start things off? Should he act like some abstract king he never knew, or should he be himself? He glanced over at Jena, who was beaming at him. What would a *real* king do? No, what would *he* do? Passing his chair, he smiled as he walked up to Sumia and the older Vulwin Elf. He extended his hand to Sumia. "Good to see you."

She motioned towards her father. "Your Majesty, may I present my father, King Faeler of the Vulwin Elves."

Realizing she wasn't going to shake his hand, he retracted it and bowed his head. "Your Majesty, thank you for coming."

Faeler had long blond hair with brown and gray highlights. He was extremely muscled, unusual for an elf. His smile was as gracious as it was dangerous. "I'm here hoping that we can rid both of our kingdoms of the Darkstriders."

Galin's face went blank.

"After I help you, will you help me?" Faeler asked.

Galin glanced over at Brock, who nodded. "Of course, we'll help you however we can, when we are able."

Faeler bowed his head. "Thank you, Your Majesty."

Galin moved over Captain Tanris and the Dwarven king, Luthur Stormtoe. "Captain, thank you for coming."

"Can't miss a planning meeting, now can I?" Tanris replied.

Luthur elbowed Tanris. "Watch your gnomish mouth when talking to a king." Luthur shook Galin's hand. "I told you the dwarves had your back."

Galin nodded. "Yes, but I didn't expect you to come, personally."

Luthur laughed. "I had to make sure that the dwarven kingdom got its fair share. I like you, but most humans aren't trustworthy."

Tanris rolled his eyes. "As if dwarves are."

Luthur glared at Tanris. "There are some races worse than humans."

"Stop it, let's get the job done, okay?"

They both nodded.

This isn't going to be easy, Galin thought. He moved over towards the elves he knew from Tadus School of Magic, the only Snow Elf and Dark Elf in room. "Nyna, Daylor, thank you for coming."

"Of course, Your Majesty," Daylor said dryly. "I can't be gone too long or I'll be missed at Staerdale Castle."

"This won't take long," Galin replied. He smiled at Nyna. "I've found the master we talked about back at school."

Daylor raised his eyebrows and leaned in.

Nyna smiled. "Was he or she able to help you?"

"Yes and no, I'll tell you later." Galin moved over towards his circle of friends, Brock, Ellis, and Mae.

"Ready to be king, Your Majesty?" Brock asked.

Galin nodded; as if he had a choice. "Let's get it done." He moved next to Jena and both of them sat at the two chairs at the head of the table. "Everyone, please be seated."

Everyone sat at the table and looked right at Galin, without saying a word.

A small black dog ran into the tent and began barking at Galin's feet. He smiled. *Is that you?*

Brock rose from the table. "I'll get it out of here."

~*Yes, it is.*~ Soreth said into Galin's mind.

Galin held his hand up. "No, it's all right."

The tiny dog began to glow. As its shape began to change, it grew taller. The canine features began to morph into . . . human. Its features sharpened. Before them stood a dark-robed, six-foot-tall human male with blue scales instead of skin, and red, glowing eyes. His hair was red and pulled back into a ponytail. "Your Majesty," Soreth said.

Everyone around the table shifted in their seats as if nervous from the sight.

Brock jumped up from the table. "What demon is this?"

Galin smiled at everyone. "Calm down, this is my teacher, Soreth. He's a blue dragon."

"That's no dragon," Faeler said as he jumped up from his seat.

Soreth licked his lips. "I've tasted Dark Elves and Vulwin Elves, they all taste the same to me."

"Soreth, enough," Galin said. "No eating my guests, please."

"As you wish . . . for now," Soreth replied.

"Everyone, please sit down," Galin said.

Jena pulled a chair from the back room and gave it to Soreth.

"Thank you, my child," Soreth said.

Galin bit his lip. He'd assembled the most diverse and diametrically opposed alliance in the history of Axain. The question now was, could he pull it all together and reclaim his kingdom? What choice did he have? "First off, I want to thank everyone for coming and aiding us in our quest to free the land from the tyranny of the Darkstriders."

"We're all with you," Luthur said.

Galin nodded. *No kidding.* He cleared his throat. "Thank you, Your Majesty. The first item is for us to figure out what our force consists of." He looked at Luthur.

"The Dwarves brought warriors, siege equipment, and miners."

"Why miners?" Brock asked.

Luthur smiled. "You never know when we might come across a vein or two. We'd give Your Majesty a royalty, of course."

Galin frowned. "We'll see."

Luthur scowled at him.

Ellis laughed.

Jena smirked.

"What's so funny?" Luthur asked.

The whole table erupted in laughter.

Luthur's face reddened. "What's so damn funny?"

"Nothing," Galin said. "Please accept my apologies."

Luthur smiled as he leaned back in his chair. "For now."

Faeler straightened up. "The Vulwin Elves brought pyromancers, warriors, and bowmen. Over five hundred elves."

Only 500? Galin swallowed. "How many dwarves did you say, Luthur?"

Luthur smiled. "Over seven hundred."

"I see," Galin said. "Nyna, any word from the Shadow Mage?"

Nyna shook her head. "None. After the school

was destroyed, all support was completely withdrawn from our cause. Even the mages who wanted to volunteer were forbidden to."

"Nothing?" Brock asked.

"Well, you have me," Nyna replied

"That's comforting," Ellis said.

Nyna glared at him.

"Father, how's our army?" Galin asked.

Brock shifted in his seat. "We have a complement of warriors, siege equipment operators, and bowmen. If you include the Feral Orcs, as well as the humans, we've got just over two thousand soldiers."

Galin stomach twisted. "Daylor, how many troops does Tanyl have?"

Daylor looked at Nyna with sad eyes. "At least ten thousand, including two battalions of war mages. We don't have enough."

Soreth's eyes glowed brighter. "Sure you do. You've got me. I'm worth at least one thousand Dark Elves."

Daylor snickered. "Really? We eliminated your kind from Setan with ease. You may be worth one hundred, but no more, I assure you."

Galin looked around the table. Every face carried the ghost of defeat before the battle had even started. His adoptive father used to tell him that a battle was won or lost long before it ever began. How could this group defeat a platoon of three-legged goblins? They couldn't.

Tanris stood up. "My flying ships can tilt the balance in our favor. We can fly over the walls, just as His Majesty suggested when he spoke with Queen Venfi."

Daylor shook his head. "No, those gnomish ships would simply be shot down by the Darkstrider's pyromancers. Everyone on those ships would die. End of story."

"We've got to take them by surprise," Galin said. He looked at Brock. "How'd they take Staerdale Castle in the first place?"

Brock cleared his throat as every eye looked upon him. "Well, they attacked Port Eldham, and the king sent the majority of the forces within the castle to defend it. When they were gone, they attacked and captured the castle. Thea the Loyal did her best, but it wasn't enough."

Daylor rubbed his chin. "I can get a small team in."

"How?" Galin asked.

"The dimensional tunnel, of course. You've used it before yourself."

Galin leaned forward. "Go on."

"I get you inside, inside the gatehouse, and you open it up. Easy," Daylor said.

"Not quite," Brock said. "There's still 10,000 soldiers inside."

"We could draw them out, just as they did before," Jena said.

"Perhaps," Daylor responded. "I'm not sure Tanyl will fall for it."

Faeler looked at Sumia. "What if it wasn't a faint?"

"What do you mean?" Daylor asked.

Sum smiled as if she figured out what her father meant. "We take Port Eldham. No ruse, we capture it. He will be forced to send his troops."

Daylor frowned. "Seriously, 500 elves? They'll never believe it. Even if they did, they'd send two thousand, at most." He glared at Sumia. "Even you must realize that. What could possibly get him to draw more troops than that?"

"Me!" Soreth said as his eyes glowed even brighter. He grinned at Daylor. "Is there a limit on how many Dark Elves I can eat?"

Daylor backed away.

"I guess the banquet is open," Ellis said with a grin.

"Will that do it?" Galin asked.

Daylor never took his eyes off Soreth. "Yes, I think so. He'd at least send most of the pyromancers to deal with the beast."

Soreth licked his lips. "I like dark meat."

"There is one more thing," Daylor said.

"What is it?" Galin asked.

"Your uncle wants to help."

Brock spit on the ground. "Kade? That bastard!"

Galin had never met his uncle, only heard stories about how he betrayed everyone. Sometimes, stories were exaggerated. Was Kade as bad as he was always told? Perhaps even the most evil of people could change. "How?"

Daylor swallowed. "He's going to kill Tanyl at the right time."

"What time is that?" Brock asked.

"After we enter the gatehouse would be the best time. The confusion might be enough tip the scales of fate in our favor," Daylor said. "You see, the Dark-striders have a rigid central leadership structure."

"So?" Ellis asked.

"So, it'll take time for them to be able to regroup," Daylor finished. He looked right at Galin. "What do you think?"

What did he think? Risky. The whole plan depended on Tanyl falling into their trap and there was no room for failure. Galin smiled. Perfect. "I love it." He rose to his feet. "Can we leave in the morning?"

Brock nodded. "Yeah, we're ready to kick their asses. I've been waiting for this a long time. Sally will be avenged tomorrow, and Thea the Loyal's sacrifice will be justified."

"Right." Galin looked into Jena's eyes. "After we are in our new home and the kingdom is freed from the Darkstriders, we'll have a baby." He kissed her forehead. "I promise."

Jena held her stomach. "I can't promise I'll wait long." She disappeared behind the curtain.

What did she mean by that? Galin followed Jena into the bedchamber.

CHAPTER 16

*B*eing in a cavern screwed with Galin's internal clock. No matter what time it was outside, it was always dark inside. His stomach growled as it demanded lunch, but it would have to remain empty, for now. Galin was packing a sack into Thea's saddlebags.

Jena was doing the same. For the first time since Galin had known her, fear fell over her face like a mask. "Can we do it?" she whispered.

Galin bit his lip. "Sure." That didn't exactly radiate with confidence, now did it. Galin's mind spun in every direction, picturing every possible outcome where they lose or end up dead. They were outnumbered. They had some experience, but not like the battle-hardened army of Feral Orcs within the castle walls. He grinned. Why was he worried? Daylor was going to get them inside, helping them open the castle gate. Brock would come inside with his army and the dwarves and swarm the Darkstriders. As long as Tanyl sent out his troops to meet Soreth and the Vulwin Elves at Port Oldham, they'd have a chance. A great chance.

"You don't sound confident," Jena said.

His eyes twinkled. "I am."

Holding Runt by the reins, Ellis approached Galin and Jena, with Mae in tow. "What are we doing with the horses?"

Galin grabbed Thea's reins. "Tanris is taking them. Come on."

Ellis, Jena, and Mae followed Galin through the lines of soldiers towards the cave mouth.

With each step, more and more of Galin's soldiers stood up and yelled, "Long live the king!" All he could do was smile. Did they know they were going to die that day? To die for . . . him? Should he say something? Was that what kings do? Was that what he would do? Yes. He passed Thea's reins off to Jena as he stepped on top of a half-loaded cart.

As Galin raised his hands, the cavern went silent. "Thank you!" He cleared his throat. "Today, we are embarking on the final step in a long journey paved with blood. Loved ones, honorable men and women, humanoids of all races, great beasts, and even Feral Orcs who've seen the light to join our cause have come together to bring freedom to the people of Axain and beyond." He glanced over at King Faeler, Sumia, and Soreth, deeper in the cavern. "There are those who stand to gain nothing, but are with us today. The world is drowning in evil and today . . . and today we're going to shine the light of Odella and rid the world of it, forever!"

The crowd cheered.

"Yeah!" Ellis screamed. "Let's kick their asses!"

Mae frowned. "You spoiled it."

Galin hopped down, grabbing the reins from Jena. "Let's go."

She kissed him on the cheek. "Now I know why I said yes."

Galin grinned. "You're just figuring it out now?"

Jena giggled.

"Jeesh, will you two ever knock it off?" Ellis said.

"No." Galin's eyes darted across the room as Daylor raced towards them. "What is it?"

Daylor's face was shining in the torchlight from the light coat of sweat on his brow. "I overslept. I've got to get back."

"Where do we wait for the tunnel?" Galin asked.

"I'll send it to inside your tent, okay?"

Galin nodded. "Do you have enough rough diamonds?"

"I do. Got to go," Daylor said as he disappeared into the crowd.

"Where to?" Mae asked.

"Back to the tent." Galin waved at Sumia as they disappeared into the lower catacombs.

"Where are they going?" Mae asked.

"This cave system is vast and there is an exit not far from the port," Brock said from behind them.

Galin whirled around.

"They'll never know what hit them," Brock finished.

"Heading out now?" Galin asked.

"Yeah, we're going to give them half a day's march before we head out."

"Why?" Mae asked. "Shouldn't you attack at the same time?"

"No, I need to give Tanyl a window to send his troops away, remember?" Brock asked.

"I guess."

"Father, good luck." Galin extended his hand to his adoptive father.

Brock pulled him in for a deep embrace. "I love

you, son. Never forget that. No matter what happens. Okay?"

"I won't."

Brock wiped away a tear from his right eye. "I've got to get ready. I'll await your signal from inside the castle."

"What signal?" Galin asked.

"When the gate comes crashing down." Brock waved as he walked towards the army's lead elements towards the cave entrance.

Ellis sighed. "Back to the tent."

Galin nodded. "Yup." He looked around. "It's going to get real lonely in here. I hate waiting."

Mae gritted her teeth as she looked right at Galin. "So do I," she muttered under her breath.

"What did you say?" Jena asked.

"Nothing."

What's she hiding? Galin thought.

SUMIA RODE her elegant black stallion next to King Faeler as they emerged from a cavern entrance just south of Nightfall Meadows. The full moon illumi-nated the forest, casting a dark shadow upon them from the enormous oak trees. A chill ran up her spine, as if it was a warning.

As soon as Soreth emerged, his figure began to blur. His human form fell onto all fours and grew larger and larger. He grew until he was at least thirty yards long and stood ten yards high. Soreth's shape transformed from a blurred blob to an elegant blue dragon. In a flash, his figure came back into focus. "I hate doing that. It's so, undignified."

"Would you scout ahead of us?" Faeler asked.

"Scout?"

"Yes, fly over Port Eldham and return to tell us what you see." Faeler sighed. "We've got a small number of troops—"

"And me."

Faeler nodded. "And you. We've got to be careful. Once you return, we can finalize our plan to attack, but we must attack within two hours or Galin will be facing the Darkstriders full force at Staerdale Castle."

"Very well," Soreth said as he took to the air.

"Father, can we trust a dragon?" Sumia asked.

"This coalition is unusual, to say the least. We've got ourselves, the humans, dwarves, gnomes, a few Feral Orcs, a beast, and even a Dark Elf." Faeler shook his head. "When I became king two hundred years ago, I never imagined that the Vulwin Elves would be working with such . . . people."

Sumia looked away and frowned. "I think it's a wonderful thing. Each race brings some unique strength that only makes us stronger. No one race is better than the other and—"

Faeler smiled at his daughter. "It's not often that a father learns from his daughter. You're right, of course."

"I only hope we can stay allies after this is all over."

"Yes, it'd be unfortunate if the Dwarves retreated back into their mines and the Gnomes hid in the north." Faeler cocked an eye at Sumia. "Perhaps this is the beginning of something new."

"Perhaps," Sumia replied. "Do you trust Daylor?"

"Changing the conversation, are we?"

"Yes. He's not only a Dark Elf, he works with Kade and Tanyl."

Faeler nodded. "Nyna trusts him, and that's good enough for me."

"Yes, Father." *I don't trust him*, Sumia thought.

WHERE DID HE GO? Kade thought to himself as he

rushed towards the Great Hall. Daylor had been missing for almost a full a day and he just . . . reappeared? Please. He must have been with them, right? Did he see his nephew? Did he tell them about his plans for Tanyl? Hopefully.

He turned a corner and pushed through the double doors. Tanyl and Daylor were sitting at the table in the center of the hall, whispering. *Is he betraying me?* "Why was I summoned like a common dog?"

Tanyl scowled at him. "Because you are one. Now sit down and do what you're told."

Kade plopped down next to Daylor. "What is it?"

"Daylor was doing his part. What about you?" Tanyl asked.

"What do you mean?"

Tanyl motioned to Daylor.

"They're going to attack," Daylor said. "Tonight."

Kade's throat went dry. Why was Daylor betraying Galin? Didn't they know each other in Tadus School of Magic? Yes, they did. Kade forced a stern face. "Go on." Kade stared at Daylor. His face was covered with sweat. Was that . . . fear?

"They're attacking Port Eldham, just like we did when we took Staerdale Castle," Daylor said.

"Why?" Kade asked. "What do they hope to gain

by separating their forces?" He blinked. "Do they have that many?"

Daylor shook his head. "No, we outnumber them."

Tanyl cocked his head as he stared right into Daylor's eyes. "How do you know this?"

"I spoke to her," Daylor replied.

"Who?" Kade asked.

Ignoring Kade, Tanyl asked, "Is our operative still with them?"

Daylor nodded. "Yes, and they don't suspect a thing. Soreth could be a problem, though."

Kade shifted in his seat. "Soreth? Who's that?" *Is he telling the truth?*

Tanyl glared at Kade. "What do you know about this?"

Kade shook his head. "Nothing. This is the first I hear of it."

"I see."

"Sorry, I don't know what to tell you."

"Get out," Tanyl said.

"But—"

Tanyl jumped from his seat. "Get out, before I have your head on a spike!"

Kade's stomach retreated into his bowels, along

with his courage. "Fine!" He slowly headed for the door, trying to hear every last tidbit he could.

"Do you have a plan?" Tanyl asked.

Daylor leaned in. "Here's what we do."

Kade slammed the door behind him. *I've got to stop that lying bastard.* He stormed off towards his chambers.

CHAPTER 17

Brock, Luthur, and Yotul rode side by side as they emerged from the woods surrounding Staerdale Castle. They moved off to the side, letting their soldiers pass by them into the field.

"They look proud," Luthur said.

Brock nodded. "Yes, they do," he said as a contingent of Dwarves pulled four trebuchets into the field.

"Do you think the Darkstriders sent their forces to face Sumia and King Faeler?"

"The attack on Port Eldham should have started four or five hours ago. If they were going to send them at all, they'd already have done so," Brock said. "Yotul, could you ride ahead and set up the siege? We need to be ready."

"Yes, sir," Yotul said as she cracked her reins.

Brock watched her ride towards the front of the column. "I can't believe it's almost over. It's been a lifetime."

Luthur frowned. "You sound sad."

"No, not sad. It's just—well, I've never done anything else but hate the Darkstriders and worked towards keeping my promise to Thea the Loyal. And now—one way or the other—it ends today," Brock said.

"As soon as Galin opens the gate, we'll take them out," Luthur said.

"I wanted to ask you about the trebuchets."

"What about them?"

"Are you going to use them after we're inside?"

Luthur laughed. "No. We'd kill more of our own people if we did that."

"Why did you bring them?"

Luthur frowned. "Just in case Galin fails. As you said, one way or the other, it ends today."

"So be it." *Odella, please look after my boy and help him succeed in his quest*, Brock thought.

"Come on, let's join Yotul. We can't let her have all the fun."

Brock smiled as he followed Luthur onto the field.

WHERE IS THAT BASTARD? Kade thought as he stormed through the corridor towards Daylor's chambers in Staerdale castle. The only Dark Elf he trusted had just betrayed his nephew, the one Daylor knew Kade wanted to save. Kade knew about Daylor's frequent trips out of the castle, including his fascination with Tadus School of Magic. Maybe Tanyl needed to know? Would that make things better or worse? Sometimes, revenge can feel good in the moment, but cause great pain in the end.

Kade flew around the corner. His eyes bore into the door ahead of him. He had to know what he'd told Tanyl. How deep was Daylor's betrayal. What if Daylor told Tanyl about his plan to kill him? Kade swallowed. No way. If he had, Kade would already be dead. No, Daylor wants something, but what? Why betray Galin? Kade unsheathed a dagger from his belt as he flung the door open.

Daylor jumped to his feet from behind his desk. "What's the meaning of this?"

Kade slammed the door shut while his eyes never left Daylor.

Daylor looked down at the dagger. "What are you going to do with that?"

Kade lunged over Daylor's desk, taking him to the ground.

Daylor's mouth began to move, speaking unrecognizable words.

"No you don't," Kade said as he punched Daylor in the mouth. He flipped the Dark Elf onto his stomach as he pulled a piece of twine from his pocket. After yanking Daylor's hands behind his back, Kade tied them up with the twine.

"What do you want?" Daylor gasped. "I thought we were friends."

"We are. That's why you're still alive," Kade said as rolled Daylor onto his back. He put the dagger to Daylor's throat. "If you start an incantation, you'll be dead before the second syllable, got it?"

Daylor nodded.

"Why did you betray my nephew?"

The blue-skinned Dark Elf's face reddened. "I betrayed? You betrayed him and his parents long ago."

"I'm fixing that now. Maybe . . . maybe he can forgive me," Kade said. He pressed the dagger against Daylor's larynx. "Why did you betray him? In case you don't know, there's an army surrounding Staerdale Castle right now. Tanyl didn't send reinforcements to Port Eldham when the Vulwin Elves attacked, so it's probably lost."

"You sound upset about that."

"I'm upset about Tanyl doing something out of character, as if he's following someone's advice. What did you tell him?"

A trickle of blood began to form on Daylor's throat under the dagger. "All right, I'll tell you, just take the dagger off my throat."

Kade returned the dagger to its sheath. "Go on."

"I just got back from being with your nephew. You should be proud of him. He's assembled a . . . unique army. Not only Vulwin Elves and humans, he's recruited Dwarves, the Gnomes with their flying ships, some Feral Orcs, and a blue dragon."

"A dragon?" Kade smiled. "How can they lose with a dragon on their side?"

Daylor frowned. "It's not as much of an advantage as you think. We vanquished hundreds of those creatures. Their weaknesses are well known to us, to Tanyl."

"So you know their plan?"

Daylor nodded. "I've got a pretty important part in it."

Kade's face darkened. "Is that what you told Tanyl?"

Daylor shook his head. "Do you realize what he'd do to me if I told that I came from a meeting with the army that wants to kill him?"

Kade put his knee on Daylor's chest, shifting all of his weight on the Dark Elf. "What did you tell him?"

Daylor gasped for air.

Kade let up a bit. "Tell me!"

"I had to give him something. He caught me as I was returning through the dimensional tunnel. So, I gave him the Vulwin Elves. They weren't crucial to Galin's plan. So what if nearly a thousand Vulwin Elves get slaughtered. I didn't tell him about the humans, the dwarves, and the gnomes that will be attacking the castle tonight. Did I mention that a dragon was coming with them?" Daylor asked.

"There're nearly ten thousand troops inside the castle. How many does Galin have?"

"Not that many, perhaps two to three thousand," Daylor said.

"He may have expected some of those troops to reinforce Port Eldham."

"Galin did." Daylor frowned. "There was no need to reinforce Port Eldham. Tanyl sent three legions of

Feral Orcs from the Tadus School of Magic to the port."

"How?"

"Magic, of course. They had several hundred mages cast Bexon's Dimensional Tunnel. They crossed the continent in a matter of seconds. When I said I gave up the Vulwin Elves, I wasn't kidding," Daylor said. "May I get up now?"

Kade rose to his feet. "Of course."

Daylor dusted himself off and picked his chair up off the floor. "You said the siege has already started?" he asked as he sat back down behind his desk.

Kade nodded. "A few hours ago. Ryul is going frantic."

"Typical of the military types, jump for action with little involved."

"How can we help Galin? You said you knew the plan," Kade said. He tapped the sheath on his belt. "If you betray him any further or if he loses, I'll kill you."

Daylor stared at the dagger. "I know."

"How do we help him?"

"Galin is waiting for a portal from me to get inside the castle, specifically into the gate house."

"Why not just fly over the walls?"

"Tsk, tsk, tsk. Our archers would simply shoot them down," Daylor replied. "You know that."

Kade leaned forward. "What do you need me to do?"

"Keep Tanyl occupied and be ready to execute your plan."

Kade nodded as he left Daylor's chambers. For a moment, he looked back at the closed door. *Can I really trust him? Where is his loyalty? To Galin or to his people?*

GALIN SIGHED as he watched Ellis roll a pebble between his fingers. They removed the large table in the center of his tent to make room for the portal. Sure, he trusted Daylor to send it, but—oh hell, he just hated the damned wait. As soon as they got to the tent, even though they knew it would be several hours, Galin and Ellis rushed to move the table and drew their weapons. The excitement overcame them. As the seconds, the minutes, and the hours passed, their adrenaline waned. What if—?

Jena snapped her fingers. "Hey, you in there?"

"Yeah, sorry," Galin replied.

"Leave him alone already," Ellis said. "Can't you

see he's fighting the battle in his head? If you can't be there in person, pretending is the next best thing."

Mae kissed him on the cheek. "My hero."

Ellis pushed her away. "Stop it. You don't believe that."

"After we're done today, I'll truly give myself to you. Completely," Mae said with a smile.

"Are you going to get married?" Galin asked.

Jena giggled.

"No," Mae said. "He hasn't asked me yet."

Ellis twirled one of his daggers in his left hand. "And I won't, either."

Mae slid her hand around Ellis's waist. "Is there anything I can do to persuade you?"

Galin rolled his eyes. For a second, the small gem on Mae's ring began to glow. *Something's not right,* he thought.

"Galin, can you go over it again?" Jena asked, obviously trying to change the subject from Mae's and Ellis's future exploits.

"Sure." Galin straightened up. "Sumia and King Faeler should have drawn some of the Darkstrider soldiers from Staerdale Castle-hopefully, most of them—and Father should have surrounded the castle by now. Daylor will open the dimensional tunnel from the gatehouse to here. We enter it and kill any guards in the gatehouse on the way to the controls."

"Easy," Mae said.

"You kind of take the fun out of it," Ellis said.

Jena's face crinkled as if in deep thought. "Why couldn't Daylor do it himself? I mean, you know the guards would see the tunnel. The gatehouse can't be much bigger than the one at Iron Fist Keep, could it?"

Galin blinked. Why couldn't Daylor do it? He popped from the castle to Tadus School of Magic and back again all the time. Surely, someone in Staerdale Castle must have seen him, after all, he's been doing it for at least two years, if not longer. No, Nyna trusted Daylor, and that was good enough for him. Nyna couldn't be wrong, right? Galin shook his head. "I'm not sure, but we're not at the castle, either."

"Have any of you been to Staerdale Castle before?" Mae asked.

"Not me," Ellis said.

Jena smiled. "I've never been to this part of Axain before."

Mae looked directly at Galin. "You?"

He looked away. "No."

"Oh," Mae said as she looked away.

"Well, at least our horses will be fed well, even if we screw it all up," Ellis said with a grin. "I'm starving myself."

Jena laughed. "All you care about is keeping your stomach happy."

Ellis pulled a muffin from his pack. "Yup," he said as he tossed it in his mouth.

Galin reached for the muffin. "Can I have—" He snapped his head to the far end of the tent. A tiny, bright, yellowish-orange light appeared three feet off the ground. "It's time," he said as he got to his feet.

Jena, Ellis, and Mae all jumped to their feet.

Galin approached the tiny light. The mere seconds he waited seemed like days. He slammed his eyes shut as a light brighter than the sun flashed from the portal. A rancid smell stung his nose as a gust of wind crashed into his face. It was there, then it was gone. He opened his eyes. The small light morphed into the dimensional tunnel they were familiar with.

Ellis held his nose. "Damn, it stinks. I don't remember that before."

Galin shrugged. "This is also the first time we weren't at the starting point."

Mae drew her sword. "Who cares? Let's go."

Ellis pulled out his daggers. "I'm ready to finish this." He beamed at Mae. "I've got a date afterwards."

"I'm ready," Jena said after she drew her short sword. "Galin?"

There would be no turning back. Once they stepped into the tunnel, they would be on their own until they brought the gate up. Did he believe in the prophecy or not? The prophecy already declared him the victor, but . . . what if it was wrong? What if he was leading his friends to their deaths all because he wanted to become king? Sure, he was doing his duty, but to be king—

Jena elbowed Galin's side. "Galin, ready?"

Galin swallowed. *This is what faith is*, he thought. He drew his sword. "Let's go." He stepped into the portal and disappeared.

CHAPTER 18

Galin squinted as he stepped out of the dimensional tunnel. The world was nothing but a blur to him. His eyes began to come into focus. They were in a small room with wooden benches along the wall and a single door on the far side. Next to the door was a tall stack of wooden crates and barrels of wine. They must be in the food stores.

"I hate those things," Ellis said, rubbing his eyes as he emerged from the tunnel.

"We all here?" Galin asked.

"Yeah," Jena said. "Me and Mae just came through."

"Good." Galin smiled as Daylor stepped into view. "Good to see you."

"Welcome to Staerdale Castle," Daylor said.

"Where are we?" Mae asked.

Daylor frowned. "Not in the gatehouse. I couldn't get inside. Ever since the attack on Port Eldham, Tanyl tightened security around it."

Ellis threw up his arms. "We're screwed! Can you get us out of here?"

Galin glared at him. "We're not done yet." He looked right at Daylor. "You know this castle. I don't. What can we do?"

Daylor rubbed his chin. "The tunnels."

"What tunnels?" Mae asked. "I never saw any tunnels here before."

Daylor gave Mae a stern gaze. "I didn't know you'd visited the castle."

Mae swallowed. "Um, yeah. When I was a kid."

Galin shook his head. "We don't have time for this."

"The tunnels your adoptive parents smuggled you out through when you were a baby. I'm sure they told you," Daylor said.

Galin nodded. "Sure. But, they can't be big enough to bring an army inside."

"No, they're not. But, they can get you out."

Galin tore his eyes away from Daylor. "I'm not

giving up. If you don't help me get the gate open, I'll do it myself."

"Maybe we should do what he says," Ellis said. "You know, live and fight another day. There's nothing wrong with that."

"You don't have to come," Galin said as he turned his back towards him.

Ellis lowered his voice. "I wouldn't have left Crey Village and gone through all this crap just to leave you at the end. No, I'll come with you."

Galin turned and smiled at his friend. "Thanks."

"Besides, somebody has to save your ass."

Galin frowned.

Jena giggled. "He always does that to you."

"Which way to the gatehouse?" Galin asked.

"If you insist, allow me to make us invisible to non-magical Dark Elves. It should aid us in getting the gate open." Daylor reached into his robes, pulling out a small pouch.

"What are you going to cast?" Jena asked.

Daylor's forehead began to glisten with sweat, as if he was nervous about . . . something. He took a large scale from the pouch and placed it in the palm of his right hand.

"What's that?" Galin asked.

"A dragon scale," Daylor said.

Dragon scale? What spell uses that? Galin thought.

Daylor waved his left hand over the dragon scale, never taking his eyes off of Galin. His mouth moved, but no sound came out. The dragon scale began to glow.

Galin felt tired, as if something was being drained out of him. "What are you doing?" He advanced towards Daylor.

Mae held him back. "Let him finish. He knows what he's doing."

A flash of light emitted from there dragon scale, then it was gone.

Gavin's vision became blurry. His . . . his heart skipped a beat. His stomach twisted into knots. He felt weak. For the first time in his life he felt . . . weak. "What have you done?" he demanded as he collapsed to the ground.

Jena rushed over to help him.

Ellis drew his daggers and charged at Daylor.

Mae stuck her foot out in front of him, sending him crashing to the ground.

"What'd you do that for?"

Mae just smiled. Her medium-length brown grew and turned black. There was a golden stripe running through her hair. Mae's ears became pointed. Her skin darkened to a deep blue. She was a Dark Elf all along, even before Iron Fist Keep.

"Chalia? How?" Galin demanded as he struggled to his feet.

The door flew open and a tall Dark Elf with short, black hair and brown eyes burst into the room, with at least six Feral Orcs carrying short swords. "Welcome, Your Majesty. I am Tanyl."

Ellis's face crumbled. "Why? I thought you loved me?"

Chalia laughed. "I used you." She glared at Galin. "Because of you, both of my parents were killed." She smiled at Jena. "I want to skin her in front of him."

Rage. The rage exploded inside Galin's heart. There was no way he'd let anything happen to his beloved. His rage was focus and pure, but—the tingle; it wasn't there. Maybe he wasn't concentrating hard enough. He tried again and again and again. Nothing.

Daylor laughed.

Galin glared at him.

"You can stop trying now," Tanyl said. "Once we figured out that you used dragon magic, we researched—Daylor researched—the spell to nullify it. You're no different than your dead father." He leaned forward. "Weak."

Tanyl looked at Jena. "Maybe I should give Chalia what she wants. What do you think, Galin?"

Galin lunged at Tanyl. A Feral Orc stepped between them, knocking him to the ground.

"It will take some getting used to, I imagine." Tanyl motioned the other Feral Orcs towards Jena and Ellis.

Galin's tearful eyes looked straight at Daylor. "How could you betray us? Betray me? Betray Nyna?"

A twisted smile stretched across Daylor's face. "Do you really believe I would ever betray my own people? Could you betray yours?"

Galin shook his head.

"What are you going to do with us?" Jena demanded.

"That depends on your army outside the gates. You see," Tanyl began, "we never sent our forces from the castle to Port Eldham. After Daylor told me your plan, I dispatched five legions of Feral Orcs to ambush your pitiful little army of Vulwin Elves. They should all be dead by now." He leaned towards Galin. "Even your blue dragon. Soon, the seven thousand troops I have will overrun your army. My forces are at least double what you have out there." He smiled as he backed away, motioning the Feral

Orcs to grab Galin. "The king wanted either my head in a box or yours. Can you guess which one it will be?"

Daylor and Chalia followed Tanyl out of the small room.

Galin tried to pull away from the orc's grasp.

He slammed the hilt of his sword onto Galin's head and his world went black.

WHY HASN'T the gate opened yet? Brock thought as he stared at the castle. He should already be inside fighting side by side with his adopted son. He looked up and down the siege line. Galin's army surrounded the castle, poised to rush inside to win the day. They were just outside of bow range from the castle, but their trebuchets could touch the Darkstriders behind the castle walls. But, the gates never opened. *Something's wrong.*

Nyna tapped Brock on the shoulder. "The gate should have been opened by now. They must have been caught—or worse."

"I was thinking the same thing," Brock said without taking his eyes off Staerdale Castle.

"Perhaps Kade turned them in after all."

Brock glared at her. "You're talking about my *son*! This is not some game that you wizards are playing, you know. You could at least *act* like you care."

She frowned. "I do care about him. I was the one who taught him how to use his dragon magic for over a year."

Brock sniffed as he motioned towards the castle. "A lot of good that did. Where is he?" His eyes began well up. "I can't lose him, too."

Nyna put her hand on his shoulder. "You won't. Have faith that the prophecy is true."

"What if it's not? What if it's just an ancient, drunk Dark Elf story?"

"Then, we have to have faith that Daylor and Galin will keep each other safe," Nyna said. She smiled. "I know it's hard, but I know we will win. Don't you feel it in your heart?"

Brock nodded. "I do. It's just—never mind. What do we do now?"

Nyna's smile vanished. "We wait and let the siege run its course. As long as the attack on Port Eldham succeeded, we'll be victorious."

"If not?"

"Reinforcements from Setan will arrive in a week or so and overrun us," Nyna replied.

Perfect, Brock thought.

CHAPTER 19

As Galin's eyelids cracked open, the torchlight from outside the bars illuminated their cell. Fog rolled through his mind like a tidal wave. He was laying down, that much he knew for sure. His head was resting on a warm lap. Struggling to focus, he looked up at a blurry, but loving face.

"He's waking up," Jena said as she pulled Galin's head into her chest. "Ellis?"

"All right, I hear you," he snapped from across the cell. Ellis's eyes were beet-red, as if he'd cried for hours.

Galin sat up and his mind's fog receded. "Where are we?" The ever-cheerful Ellis was no more. Even in the worst times, Galin never saw him cry. Could he blame him? No. How would Galin feel if Jena turned out to be a Dark Elf? How would he feel if he unknowingly aided the Darkstriders, betraying his friends? Awful, that's how he'd feel. No doubt. He smiled at Jena. Well, at least they'd be together in the end. Thank Odella that Jena was not pregnant. Perhaps it was a blessing from the gods to spare an unborn child from the torment they were certain to go through and eventually perish from. Galin struggled to his feet and walked over to Ellis.

"I'm glad you're all right," Ellis said. "We won't be for long, you know."

Galin nodded and smiled at his old friend. "I know." He plopped down next to Ellis. "We need your crazy ideas on how to get out of here."

Jena moved over next to Galin. "Yeah, Ellis, we can't die in here. Help us." Her eyes began to well up.

"It's all right, Jena. We'll make it," Galin said. *Liar!*

A forced smile fought its way across Jena's tearful face. She nodded. "I know we will."

"Where are we in the castle?"

Ellis wiped the tears from his face. "We seem to be on the lowest level in the castle. Tanyl was describing how many different ways he was going to kill us the whole way down. Mae—I mean that bitch, Chalia—joined in."

"I see." Galin looked around. To the left and to the right was another cell. Outside the bars was a small walkway heading out the doors. Torches were mounted in sconces along the wall. The wooden door appeared impervious. Well, it was, as long as they were behind bars. They had to get out.

"How do we get out?" Jena asked.

"They took my picks," Ellis said. "Chalia knew right where to find them."

Galin frowned. How many other secrets were betrayed by Chalia? What else did she know? Everything. How come he didn't figure it out? What clues did he miss? The ring! Yes, her ring glowed whenever Galin and Ellis were fighting or . . . whatever. A magic ring? Had to be. "It's not your fault."

"Yes, it is," Ellis said.

"No, Chalia had a ring that glowed every time we got into an argument or when she wanted you to do something that you didn't. No, it wasn't your fault."

"Whatever." Ellis tore his eyes away.

"Ellis, how do we get out of here?" Jena asked.

Galin smacked Ellis in the shoulder. "Snap out of it. Do you want to live?"

Ellis nodded.

"Then help us get out of here, before it is too late," Galin said.

Ellis wiped the tears from his eyes. "Well, assuming that we can get out of this . . . cage, the door is our next major obstacle." He rubbed his chin and stared at the door, as if recalling something. "I don't remember them locking the door. You'd have heard it if they did."

"Our only chance is to open the gate so my father can bring the troops inside."

Jena rubbed her belly. She stared at Galin with a fearful face.

"What is it?" Galin asked.

As if on cue, Jena's mouth opened and vomit spewed from her mouth all over Galin.

"What the?" Ellis said as he jumped up.

Galin looked down at his puke-covered clothes.

"I'm sorry," Jena said as she wiped away the vomit from his clothes. "I don't know what happened."

"Nerves?" Galin asked.

Jena frowned. "Sure. Nerves."

Was he missing something? Maybe. It would be better to change the subject, right? Yeah. "After we get out, we'd have to get some weapons and fight our way to the gatehouse."

"No," Ellis said.

"No?"

"Yes, I said no. That's a stupid plan," Ellis said. "They'd overrun us in seconds and we'd be right back here again. If that happened, I'd throw up on you, too."

Jena looked down at the ground.

Galin patted her leg. "It's okay. It happens."

"How would you do it?" Jena asked.

"Well, we kill three soldiers and take their clothes. Then, we walk from the castle to the gate-house, acting like we belong there. Then, we open the gate. Simple," Ellis said with a smile.

Galin frowned. "I doubt it's that simple."

"Better than your lousy plan. At least we *survive* in mine."

Jena rolled her eyes. "He's back."

"Fine," Galin said. "How do we—"

The door flew open and slammed against the wall. Five Feral Orcs wearing chain mail armor came into the dungeon. They opened the cell and motioned to Jena. "You, come with us."

Jena slowly got to her feet.

"No!" Galin stepped between Jena and the orcs. "Take me instead, she is no value to you."

The front orc backhanded Galin, knocking him to the ground. "Weak human." He grabbed

Jena's arm.

"Where are you taking me?" Jena demanded.

"To the seers. They want to talk to you."

The seers? They torture—no, they mutilate anyone they question. Even Yotul feared them. "No!" Galin charged at the orcs.

Two more orcs grabbed his arms, holding him in front of the lead Feral Orc.

The orc leaned in. "If she's lucky, the baby she's carrying will die. No telling what will happen to the child if it survives the magical interrogation." It punched Galin in the stomach, sending him reeling to the ground.

Pain. Which was worse, his stomach or Jena not telling him? "Is it true?" Galin asked Jena.

Jena looked away.

"Of course it is," Ellis said. "Everyone knew it but you."

"Jena?"

She nodded.

"Why didn't you tell me?" Galin demanded.

"I . . . I tried," Jena said through the tears.

The orc wrenched her out of the cell. "Come on."

"Please, please don't. My baby! My baby!" Jena screamed as she was dragged out of the dungeon.

Galin watched the door slam shut. *What have I done?*

HOW COULD Galin have been so blind? It seemed like hours since they took Jena away. Galin looked over at Ellis. Now, he truly understood how Ellis must feel. No, Jena didn't betray him; he betrayed her by not truly *hearing* her. Sure, he couldn't take hints very well. In fact, Jena told him many times that he wouldn't recognize what she was saying unless she hit him over the head with it. Why didn't she tell him? It wasn't a small thing.

Galin's mind drifted back. Yeah, she did try to tell him. When she asked about having children, he always said no. Did she know that she was pregnant then? Galin shook his head. No. Maybe? Perhaps? No. Maybe he made her feel too uncomfortable to tell him because of his attitude? Yeah, that was it. He should have been the supportive husband and not think of his own pleasure first. Life would change with a new baby and he knew it. Galin glanced over at the door, praying that it would open. It didn't.

"I should've told you," Ellis said. "I can't sit in silence anymore."

Galin glanced over at his friend. "I can't either. Why didn't you tell me? You knew, right?"

Ellis nodded. "Both me and Mae—I mean Chalia, knew. I didn't tell you because you never wanted to talk about it. That's why Jena kept it a secret, too."

It is my fault, Galin thought. Would he be good father? Like Brock? Or would he try to become the father he never knew? Maybe he never wanted to discuss it because—oh hell, he just didn't want to hear it and he knew it. He made his choice when he and Jena made love the many times after they were married. An act of love doesn't result in "consequences," it brings about the personification of their love. A child. Could he a be—

"Don't be too hard on yourself. She's only two months along. You'll make it up to her," Ellis said.

"If we survive this," Galin replied.

Ellis frowned. "That's the first time I've heard you say that things are hopeless. We've been captured before and we always get out of it, *somehow.*"

"How do we get out of this one? We can't even get out of this *damn* cage! Jena is being tortured right now by the seers. Do you remember what Yotul said about them? Even the orcs are fearful of them. She could lose the baby . . . or worse, she could die. I can't deal with that."

Ellis rushed over towards Galin and kicked him in the side, knocking him over. "Well, you have to deal with it, you son of a bitch!"

"Why'd you do that?" Galin demanded.

"Are you going to deal it with it now? We followed you because we believe in you. Now, when things get a little tough—"

"A little?"

"Yeah, a little. When things get a little tough, you want to roll over and cry in the corner. Well, boo hoo. Poor, poor Galin." Ellis's face darkened. "How many people died for you to become king? How many people were tortured to death for you? Did you ever think of that? How will you tell their families that their sacrifice wasn't good enough to motivate you to, at least, try to do what you promised? Do you even believe in freedom from tyranny? From the Darkstriders?"

"Of course I do."

"Then do it. Shut up about it and do it." Ellis plopped down next to his friend. "Besides, I'm going to kill that bitch and I don't want you screwing it up."

Galin smiled. "I—"

The door flew open, slamming against the wall with a loud bang. Four Feral Orcs dragged Jena's lifeless body inside the room and tossed her into the cell. As soon as she hit the floor, Jena let out a moan.

"Jena!" Galin rushed to her side, quickly looking over her body. There were no marks or—

Jena's eyes cracked open. As soon as she saw Galin, tears flowed down her cheeks. "I'm so sorry. I couldn't help it."

He pulled her into his chest, hugging her with all of his soul. "I'm here. It's okay. I'm here." Galin started to rock her back and forth in his arms. "Are you all right?"

"I . . . I . . . I think so. But, I . . . I told them everything. I couldn't help it," Jena said as she tore her eyes away from him. "I'm so sorry."

"Shhh, just rest now. It doesn't matter now," Galin said.

"The seers got into my mind and . . . and all my nightmares came true." Her pleading eyes latched onto his. "They made me believe that my nightmares were true and only they could protect me against them. They made me believe that my baby—"

Galin smiled. "Our baby. I'm so sorry. I was too thick to hear what you were trying to tell me."

"I love you."

"I see no bruises or cuts or anything on your body."

Jena shook her head. "No, they attacked my mind, nothing more. I can't imagine anything being worse than that."

Galin glanced down at her stomach. "Think he's all right?"

"What makes you think it's a boy?" Jena asked with a smile.

"I . . . I don't know."

"It has to be a boy," Ellis said. "He needs an heir to the throne. If he ever gets to be king."

"Why does it have to be a boy?" Jena asked.

Galin kissed her. "Let's worry about that later. I'm so happy to have you back. We'll raise *our* child to be better than the both of us."

"You mean it?"

"I do."

"What about not giving up what we already have?"

He kissed her forehead and patted her stomach. "We're not. We're just moving to the next step in our journey of love."

"Oh please!" Ellis said as he turned away in disgust.

"We have to get out of here first," she said.

"We will. I promise. Now get some sleep," Galin replied. He looked down at Jena resting on his lap with a smile on her face. *How the hell am I going to do that?*

CHAPTER 20

Galin frowned as he choked down the gruel the guards brought them for dinner. Sure, he didn't like it when Sally used to make it for him, but that was before she was . . . murdered by the Dark Elves. He glanced at Jena and Ellis, who were just as unimpressed with their cuisine. A tear flowed down his cheek. He promised to get them out, but how? He didn't want to see Ellis die, but if he had to choose whom to save, he'd save Jena. Galin shook his head. No, he'd save them both. Somehow, he'd save them both.

Galin's head jerked up as the door opened. A man with graying blond hair and sagging eyes stepped inside. Unlike the guards, an aura of confidence surrounded him, and yet sadness overtook him. *Who's that?*

The man looked right at Galin and frowned. "Galin?"

Galin nodded.

"I'm Kade, your uncle," he said. "I'm sorry about this."

Galin's face reddened. "So many people died because of you." He turned away. "If you've come here to gloat, don't bother."

"Why'd you do it?" Jena asked. "The stories about you are horrible."

"Yeah," Galin said. "They say that you murdered your brother and his queen for the throne. You murdered Galin's mother and father. How could you do that? How evil does one have to be?"

"Simple," Ellis began, "he's a jerk, lower than ogre dung."

Kade bit his lip. "Yes, I made . . . mistakes."

"Mistakes?" Galin demanded. "You betrayed your kind. Some would call that treason."

"All right, it's all true. But, Beldroth controlled me with her stupid ring," Kade said.

Ellis blinked. "A ring?"

Kade looked right at him. "Yes, a ring. Just like the one Chalia used on you, my boy." He focused his eyes back on Galin. "I want to help you, with all of it. Daylor betrayed us all."

Galin frowned. "What do you mean us?"

"I was going to help you, but he betrayed me . . . and you."

"How did he betray you?" Ellis asked. "We're in here and you're out there."

"I . . . I went to him about killing Tanyl when you attacked and he agreed to help me. You see, the Dark Elves and the Feral Orcs are miserable here. They want to go home to Setan, not occupy Axain," Kade said.

Galin shrugged. "Looks like you got out of your insurrection easily."

"Wait a minute,'" Jena said. "If he betrayed your plan for killing Tanyl, why aren't you in prison with us?"

Kade looked away. "I don't know. I can't figure out what he's really up to. Daylor told me that he was caught returning from your planning meeting and had to give Tanyl something. As soon as I found out that Beldroth's daughter was disguised as a human in your party feeding information back to Tanyl, I knew he'd played me like a fool."

"If what you say is true, why are you still alive?

The Darkstriders are not known for their leniency," Galin said.

"I don't know." Kade shook his head. "I didn't come here to talk about me. I came to meet the man whom I briefly knew as an infant. I came to meet the man who sent the Darkstriders into irrational fear of a boy-king."

"Great, you've met me. Now what?"

Kade face went white. "I . . . I don't know."

"Can you get us out of here?" Ellis asked.

"No, I can't," Kade replied. "There's no way to get past the guards. Unless—are any of you wizards? Like Daylor?"

"No," Galin said. "I can't use that kind of magic." He stared at Kade's tortured face, looking as if there was a battle going on inside his head. "What are you not telling us, uncle?"

"You're being executed in the morning." Kade looked away.

"There's more, isn't there?"

Kade nodded. "Yes. The attack on Port Eldham failed. Sumia and King Faeler were both captured."

"The dragon?"

"Escaped."

"So he's alive?"

Kade nodded. "For now. Even though Brock has

the castle under siege, reinforcements are on the way here as we speak. As soon as they arrive, the gates will open and eight thousand troops will pour out of the castle and kill everyone you've ever loved."

Jena tugged at Galin's arm. "Forget about that, we've got to get out of here. Remember, our baby?"

Kade blinked. "Baby?"

"Yes, she's pregnant," Galin said. "I . . . I just found out. If you really want to help, you'll help us get out of here and open the gate before the reinforcements arrive. I—" He stopped as a mind touched his. The dragon must be close.

~You're betrayed,~ Soreth whispered into Galin's mind.

Galin closed his eyes. *Where are you?*

~Close. I'm above the castle, amongst the clouds.~

"What's going on?" Kade demanded. "What's wrong with him?"

"This is the normal Galin," Ellis said. "Weird."

Jena frowned. "Ellis, stop it."

Can you help us? They're executing us tomorrow.

~No, not yet. But, as soon as the opportunity arises, I will.~

Fair enough. Galin opened his eyes. "How are we being executed tomorrow?"

"What the hell just happened?" Kade demanded.

"Was that Soreth?" Jena asked.

"Yes," Galin said.

"Who's Soreth?" Kade asked.

"The dragon," Galin replied. "We can talk with our minds. I don't fully understand—"

"Hold on," Jena began. "Don't you use dragon magic to talk to him?"

"Yeah."

"How's that possible if Daylor's spell nullified your magic?"

"It shouldn't be." How was that possible? Galin shouldn't have been able to speak with Soreth's mind, right? Was it some kind of trick? Sure, Chalia knew that he could speak to the dragon's mind, but why bother? Why expend the energy? No, it felt right. It felt like Soreth. Could this be part of the Transformation? "Jena, I need to tell you something."

"What?"

"Soreth told me that dragons go through the Transformation when they attain a certain amount of dragon magic."

"What's that?"

Galin swallowed. "Their power increases exponentially. But, he said that he never saw a human with dragon magic like me. He said that I could get great power or, or, mostly likely, I'll die. You see, dragon bodies are built to withstand the stresses their magic puts on the body. Humans aren't."

"Why are you telling us this?" Ellis asked.

"Maybe it started. Maybe that's why Daylor's spell is fading," Galin said.

"Maybe you're just nuts."

Galin frowned. "You're such a jerk."

Ellis grinned at him.

"You can use your magic now?" Kade asked.

"I'm not sure. I can't fight yet, I know that for sure."

Kade turned toward the door. "I can't help you escape, not now. I'm sorry." He closed to the door behind him as he left the dungeon.

"Why didn't you tell me before?" Jena asked.

Galin hugged her. "I didn't want you to worry. I love you."

"How do we get of here?" Ellis said.

Galin's face fell. "I don't know. I just don't know."

Brock stared at the castle wall before them. It almost felt like he'd come home . . . almost. If only Sally and Keya were there with him, he'd feel a lot more confident. Both women had that effect on him.

Maybe that's what love does to every man. He sighed as his eyes scanned the wall. Torchlight could be seen in all four towers. The ones on the corners seemed to have no one on top. Soldiers, pyromancers, and others crowded on top of the two towers on either side of the gate. Yeah, their job was to stop any attempt to break through the gate. He gazed up at the stars. *Odella, please look after my boy.* Trebuchets, siege equipment, and soldiers of nearly every race surrounded the castle. It nearly reminded Brock of when the Darkstriders attacked the castle, but he was on the wall. Yeah, it nearly felt like he'd come home. Brock felt a tug on his tunic and looked down to see Luthur and Tanris by his side. "What is it?"

"Everything is ready—to siege the castle, I mean."

Brock sighed. "All right."

Nyna joined them. "Any word from Sumia or King Faeler?"

Brock shook his head. "I have to assume they were victorious. Right?"

"We can still fly over the walls, can't we?" Tanris asked.

"I—"

"No," Nyna said. "We have to give this plan a chance to work."

"As I remember, there's a whole town inside the castle walls. It's a good two hundred yards to the castle itself. Well, from this side of it, anyway," Brock said. "I'm worried about Galin . . . and the others, too."

Whoosh. Whoosh.

Brock looked up. "Soreth."

The huge blue dragon circled above them and quickly descended.

"Watch out!" Tanris shouted as he dove out of the dragon's way.

Soreth reared back as his feet touched the ground. "It's done."

Brock stared at him. Scorch marks covered Soreth's body. "Are you all right? What happened?"

Soreth sneered at Staerdale Castle. "They ambushed us."

"Sumia? King Faeler?" Nyna asked.

Soreth's eyes turned red. "Captured. All of them. We were outnumbered five to one, at least. That wasn't the worst of it."

Brock raised an eyebrow. "Go on."

"They seemed to know our plan better than we did."

Nyna rubbed her chin. "Dark Elves have a lot of power, but they can't read minds."

Soreth shook his head. "No, Sumia believed we were betrayed. That was . . . just before they decapitated her. Port Eldham is still in their hands." The dragon lowered his head. "I failed you. I failed Galin."

Luthur looked straight up into Soreth's eyes. "You did. But, don't let it get you down. I'm sure you'll screw up more tonight," he said with a smile.

Soreth growled.

"Nyna, you said we had a week before reinforcements could arrive, right?" Brock asked.

Nyna nodded. "If they're coming from Setan. If they're coming from Port Eldham, maybe hours."

Tanris cleared his throat. "There's only thing we can do, and we don't have much of a choice about it."

"What?" Luthur demanded.

"Retreat, of course. Fight another day."

Luthur punched Tanris in the head, sending him to the ground. "We can always count on the pacifist Gnomes to run away," he snorted. "We can't leave Galin now, can we?"

Tanris rubbed the back of his head as he got to his feet. "I suppose."

What cowards! Why did Galin bring them? Brock thought. "We're not leaving them." What could they do?

"I spoke to Galin," Soreth said. "He's alive and in their dungeon, for now."

"How?" Nyna asked. "How'd you speak to him?"

"Dragons can communicate with one another through our magic. He told me that they're going to be executed in the morning." Soreth lowered his head, staring right at Brock. "We don't have much time."

"How?" Nyna demanded.

Brock sighed as he looked right at Tanris. "We fly over the walls and open the gate."

"Now? No. I need to find Daylor and figure out what the hell is going on. Excuse me," Nyna pushed her way past Brock, heading into the night.

Luthur started after her.

Brock grabbed him by the shoulder. "No, let her go. We need you."

Luthur nodded. "Okay. What's the plan?"

Brock pointed to one of the many trebuchets surrounding the castle. "We bombard them throughout the night. We keep them up all night, while most of our force gets some sleep. We—"

Soreth belched.

Brock held his nose as the dragon's foul breath smacked him in the face. "Really? A dragon burp? You act like my son, when he was twelve."

"Excuse me," Soreth said. "Continue, please."

"At dawn, we have a force fly over the wall, near the gatehouse, and let the rest of us in," Brock said.

"I'll help you get over the wall," Soreth said.

"You're going to let him ride you?" Tanris asked.

Soreth spit on the ground. "Do you really believe that I would let a *human* ride me like they do a horse? Please. I meant I will give them some cover from the soldiers on the wall."

"I'll have my people start the bombardment," Luthur said. "Be ready by first light."

Brock smiled at the soldiers on top of the castle walls. "We will."

DAYLOR SMILED to himself as he navigated through the corridors towards his chambers. For the first time in over fifteen years, his conscience was clear. No more pretending that he hated the Darkstriders. No more pretending that he was the ultimate betrayer of his people. No, no more. Ever since his sister, Beldroth, asked him to watch over her husband and daughter, he began to question his decision to take on the special mission from the Dark Elf king. No one, not even Tanyl, knew about his mission. Why should he? After all, Daylor was promised not just Axain, but the whole continent if he thwarted the prophesied outcome, if he saved the Dark Elves from the mythical boy-king. Myth? Perhaps, but those around Galin believed it. Tanyl believed it. Heck, even Galin's own family believed it. Why not claim his mission accomplished and be done with it? Human males cannot use magic, got it, but so what? Even once in a while nature makes a mistake. No, he proved the boy wasn't this mythical boy-king because he now sits in his dungeon with his powers suppressed. No, he'd won.

Daylor pushed open the door and stepped inside his chambers. When he saw Nyna sitting on the edge of his bed, he frowned. "You shouldn't be here," Daylor said as he closed the door.

Nyna lunged at him, pinning him against the door. "You were supposed to get them into the gatehouse and open the gates. What happened? Where is Galin?"

Daylor pushed her away. "In the dungeon. If it wasn't for me, he'd be dead right now. A little gratitude." Did he really need to keep this up? He forced out a tear. "Kade betrayed us all. I was too trusting. Forgive me."

Nyna's face softened. "I'm . . . I'm sorry. I—well, we didn't hear from you and I thought—"

"That I betrayed you? How could you? After all the years we've known each other?" He slid his right hand under his robes.

Nyna embraced him. "I remember what you said last year, when I was training Galin."

Daylor nodded as he slipped a dagger behind Nyna with his right hand and hugged her. "I said I loved you, right before we made love."

"I'm so scared for them. But . . . but I feel safer with you. I feel like we can't lose." Her tearful eyes looked into his. "Do you still love me?"

Daylor plunged the dagger into her back.

She screamed.

"No, I never did," he said as he tossed her to the floor like a piece of refuse. Daylor yanked the dagger out, straddling her chest.

"How . . . how could you?"

He slammed the dagger into her throat. "Because I'd never betray my own people, any more than you could betray yours!"

Nyna's eyes rolled back into her head.

Daylor wiped the dagger off with Nyna's robes. *We don't have much time.* He had to find Tanyl!

CHAPTER 21

I'm not a dog that can be summoned like the piss boy! Kade thought as he stormed through the double doors into the Great Hall.

Tanyl stood frowning in front of the throne with Daylor at his side. Ryul entered the room with Darkstrider knights, blocking any chance of escape.

Kade saw Ryul grinning. *Not good.* "Why have I been summoned?"

"Daylor told me a cute little story. Want to hear it?" Tanyl asked.

Kade shook his head.

Ryul grabbed him by the shoulders, forcing him to sit at the large table in the center of the room.

I have to use my wits, Kade thought. He smiled. "Thank you for getting my chair, Ryul. I never knew you were so cordial." He motioned to Tanyl. "Please, I love a good story." *They're going to kill me.*

"I understand that you plan to kill me," Tanyl said. "Is that true?"

What do I say? He obviously knows the answer. Kade smiled at Daylor. "Yes, it is. When Daylor came to me with the idea, why wouldn't I? Your close, personal advisor must have a good reason for it, especially when he came to me with the idea." He leaned forward. "What would you do, Tanyl?"

Daylor's mouth hit the floor as Tanyl glared at him. "I didn't . . . I swear, he came to me."

"Kade, why would Daylor betray me? It seems like you'd say anything to save your skin," Tanyl said.

It's working. Kade nodded. "Yes, and so would you. But, I know you're going to kill me anyway. So, why bother? You don't have a reputation for forgiveness to humans—or to Dark Elves, for that matter."

Daylor swallowed. "Kade, it's over."

Kade laughed. "Really? The castle is under siege and they have a dragon on their side. You can't leave Port Eldham unguarded until reinforcements arrive and you can't just run outside to fight them because you risk them getting inside the castle. Not to mention that they've been bombarding the castle walls all night. Hell, they could be through those walls before sunrise." *What a bunch of crap!* He studied Tanyl's quivering face. "You know what I say is true, Tanyl"

A thin smiled slithered across Daylor's face. "Not quite. You do know Shadow Mage? Yes?"

Kade blinked. "The Sorceress?"

"Yes."

"I do, so what? She's neutral in this, always has been."

"She was given a . . . proposal that she couldn't turn down," Tanyl said.

What the hell are they talking about? Kade thought.

"While *our* forces kill Galin's dragon and the rest of his pitiful army, she's sending five hundred necromancers with their . . . pets to attack them from behind," Daylor said. "It's going to be beautiful, don't you think?"

Kade shook his head. "What do you mean . . . pets?"

"Liches," Tanyl answered. "It was Daylor's idea, some six months ago."

Kade's heart nearly stopped. Daylor was planning this all along! His stomach twisted as he finally realized that he was played for a fool by the Dark Elves once more. "They'll be killed."

Daylor smiled. "Worse. They'll become liches themselves."

"A fitting end to your family, don't you think?" Tanyl asked. "And you're wrong, we're not going to kill you, yet."

"Why not?"

"I still need a human face for ruling the kingdom, for now. But, if I hear any more rumors of betrayal, you'll become a lich yourself, understand?" Tanyl demanded.

Kade's eyes fell to the floor. What choice did he have? As a lich or in the cell next to them, how could he help Galin? He wouldn't. Kade was going to die tonight, but he'd make sure it was a good death. "I understand." *I can't wait until I slit his throat with his own dagger!*

Sunlight crept through the small barred window, tugging at Galin's eyelids. He yawned. Yeah, today he was going to die. He promised Jena that he'd figure something out, but he couldn't think of anything. Wing it? He snickered to himself. Did he really have a choice? Perhaps Kade would help them, maybe?

Galin felt a faint tingle from his heart. It was like

the tingle when he summoned his dragon magic but different, somehow. He hadn't brought on horrific images; no it was more . . . constant. More natural, maybe? Was this the beginning of the Transformation? Well, that ruled out one of the three possibilities. What was left? The Transformation would either kill him or . . . mature his powers. Galin looked down at Jena, sleeping on his chest. If it killed him, she would be destroyed. They have to survive the day first, then he could worry about it later. He'd have to wait for the right moment, when his powers returned a little more. He stroked Jena's hair.

The door burst open. Tanyl, Daylor, Chalia, and four guards came through the door.

Galin, Jena, and Ellis jumped up.

A smile stretched across Tanyl's face from ear to ear. "It's time to end this false prophecy."

Tears streamed down Jena's face. "Please don't. Please don't. I don't want to die."

Chalia licked her lips. "Is this how a priestess of Odella is supposed to act?"

Jena looked away.

"Leave her alone, Chalia," Galin said.

"I still love you," Ellis said, staring at Chalia. "Even though you betrayed us all."

Galin glared at Ellis. "She's using the damn ring again."

"No, I'm not," Chalia said. "Why should I? When you are all going to be executed today. Ellis, you were fun to be around, but that was it. You were a nice pet to me, nothing more."

"I'm going to kill you!" Ellis shouted.

"Doubtful."

Tanyl crossed his arms and stared at them like a father disciplining his kids. "Children, please. No more fighting. Let them die with dignity."

"I look forward to that," Chalia said.

Galin stared at Daylor. Did he suspect that his spell was wearing off? "Nyna will avenge us and kill you."

Daylor tugged at his chin. "Oh, I forgot to tell you. I killed her, so . . . she will not avenge you."

"What? When?"

"Does it really matter?" Daylor gave a tired glance at Tanyl. "What are we waiting for? The sooner we place their heads on the wall, the sooner this wretched siege will end."

Nyna dead? No, can't be. Why would he lie? He wouldn't. Not now. "You will pay with your life, Daylor," Galin said.

"Not likely."

Tanyl motioned to the guards. "Get them out of here."

"Yes, sir," one of the guards said as they grabbed Jena, Galin, and Ellis by the arms.

"Let's go," Tanyl said as he left the dungeon.

Where's my uncle? Galin thought.

The guards dragged the trio out the door, following Tanyl.

After navigating through the corridors within Staerdale Castle, they emerged onto the courtyard. Galin squinted his eyes, trying to block the blinding sunlight. He blinked. His nose itched from the smoke from the burning, demolished buildings inside the walls. Did his forces do this? Yes. Had to be.

"Incoming!" a guard yelled from the tower.

Galin's eyes widened as a flaming stone flew over the wall, decimating a small house. The flames spread. The people screamed. Human and Dark Elf a like. This was the ugliness of war, of his quest for the throne. Was it worth it? He glanced over at Jena, sobbing quietly. Her life was worth it. Their baby was worth it.

"As soon as they see your head, this carnage will stop," Tanyl said.

Galin closed his eyes. *Come on, damn you!* The slight tingle grew and grew and . . . withdrew back into his heart. Damn it! I can't fail now. *No, not now!* He looked up. Just ahead was a platform with three raised logs on top. They were notched in such a way that . . . a person's hands and head would be secured to—.

"Did you hear me?"

"What are you doing?" Daylor demanded. He frowned. "He's trying to use his dragon magic."

Tanyl waved him off. "Don't be stupid. You surpassed it, remember?"

Daylor nodded. "Kade's by the platform. Do we need to worry?"

Tanyl pointed to the enormous Dark Elf standing next to Kade. "With Ryul right next to him? No. Besides, once his nephew is dead, isn't it honorable for the uncle to follow suit?"

Daylor grinned. "I can't wait."

Ellis looked up at Chalia, but she wouldn't return his glance. He turned away.

"Are you sure you are not fulfilling the prophecy by killing us?" Galin asked.

"Be silent, boy. You know nothing about *our* prophecy," Tanyl said.

"Perhaps I unite the world against you in death.

Perhaps, your trophy is what destroys the Darkstriders, not my little revolution," Galin said.

Daylor smacked Galin in the back of the head. "Shut it."

The guards led Galin, Jena, and Ellis up the stairs along the side of the platform. Galin swallowed as the guard forced him onto his knees. A loop came out of the log, where both ends burrowed into the log on either side of the large notch. This was it.

"Get down there!" the guard said as he slammed Galin's neck into the notch. He slipped the loop over Galin's neck and yanked the rope tight.

"Ahh!" Galin felt the rope tearing into his flesh, immobilizing his neck. His eyes looked up to see his uncle, Kade.

Kade's eyes welled up and his face twisted, as if trying to hold back a cracked dam. "I'm with you."

Ryul smacked him on the shoulder. "What did you say?"

"I'm trying to comfort my nephew. Do you mind!?" Kade demanded.

Ryul growled at him.

Tanyl, Daylor, and Chalia joined them. "Ah, Kade, glad to see you made it," Tanyl said. "Did you make the preparations I asked for?"

Kade nodded. "Most of the forces are near the wall."

Why are they doing that? Galin thought.

"As soon as Brock's forces throw up a white flag to retrieve the bodies, we'll charge out and overrun them. They'll never know what hit them," Ryul said.

Tanyl licked his lips. "Brilliant."

Galin bit his lip. It was all his fault. Everyone who followed him would die and, even after death, it was still his fault. His tearful eyes glanced over at Jena. "I'm sorry. I'm so, so sorry."

Jena swallowed a sob. "It's okay. At least we are together." Her free hand reached for him.

Galin took it and squeezed. "I love you. I love you with all my life."

"I love you, too."

"Enough of that crap," a guard said as he smacked their hands away. "Do I need to tie them up?"

Ryul shook his head. "I want to see them squirm."

A female Feral Orc carrying a two-handed battle ax with an ornate handle walked up the stairs onto the platform. Her chain mail was polished as if it was more ceremonial than for combat.

Galin looked into her eyes. They seemed . . . sorrowful. No, not possible. Why would an executioner care about the ones she was going to execute? She wouldn't unless . . .

~Stay on the platform.~ Soreth said to Galin's mind.

Are you here?

~Not, yet. But, <u>we're</u> coming.~

Hope! It almost made Galin smile. He just had to survive a few more minutes. He blinked. Did the executioner wink at him? He could only see her out of the corner of his eye. Galin couldn't quite make out the face. Could it be . . . Yotul?

Tanyl leaned forward. "Do you have any last words you want us to give your adoptive father? Before we gut him?"

A few minutes. He could do it. This was his chance. Galin struggled to look Tanyl in the eyes. "Yes."

"Well, go on then."

"Incoming!" a guard called out from the wall. The fiery projectile slammed into one of the three enormous water towers, spilling all the water onto the guards below.

Whoosh. Whoosh.

"Dragon!" the guard yelled.

Soreth swooped down, picking up the guard with his talons. He flew towards another water tower, slamming the Dark Elf into it, knocking it over.

Daylor stepped back. "That's a blue dragon!"

"So?" Tanyl said. "It's breath is a weapon. The ground is sopping wet. Get inside the castle. Run!"

Ryul drew his axes as he watched Tanyl, Daylor, Chalia, and several guards run towards the castle entrance. "Cowards!" He looked up at the executioner. "Do it! Do it, now!"

Soreth knocked over the last water tower, drenching several thousand Darkstrider soldiers. In midair he reeled back his head, as if taking a deep a breath.

Galin squeezed his eyes shut. At least it would be over quickly.

The ax slammed onto the log, right next to Galin's head, severing the rope. "I don't take orders from you!" Yotul yanked her ax from the log and leaped onto Ryul.

Kade jumped onto the platform, freeing Jena and Ellis. "Yotul, get up here, now!"

Soreth exhaled, blowing lightning from his mouth. All the Darkstriders that were still in the courtyard screamed. Electrical arcs jumped up from the sopping ground and electrocuted anyone not on the wooden platform.

In unison, the screams stopped. Galin looked up. Yotul was dead. The Feral Orc who joined him at Iron Fist Keep gave her life for a human. *She will be remembered.* "Are you on our side?" Galin asked.

"How do you think they got in?"

"They?" Ellis asked.

Kade pointed up into the sky. Ten Gnome flying ships flew over the walls. Ropes dropped down from their sides and Galin's fighters slid down to the ground.

"Is it safe to get off here?" Galin asked.

Kade nodded.

"Let's go."

"Wait!" Kade pulled Galin's sword from his hilt. "You're going to need this. A king must have a royal sword and the honor to wield it. All I ask is to let me help you set things right."

"For what?' Ellis asked. "All of this is your fault!"

Kade nodded. "It is. I ask for nothing in return."

"Fine. Let's go." Galin ran towards the gate. With each step, the stench of burnt bodies seared his nostrils. He could do it! A familiar figure stood just outside the gatehouse. It was Brock! He ran towards his adoptive father. "Father!"

Brock hugged him. "I was so worried. I thought you were . . . dead."

"Almost."

Brock glared at Kade. "What's he doing here?"

"He helped us, just like Daylor said he would."

Brock's hand tightened around the hilt of his sword. "So? He's guilty for the death of your parents, Sally, Thea the Loyal, and Odella only knows how many others. We should kill him right here."

Galin grabbed his adoptive father. "No! Because he's my uncle."

Kade stood motionless. His mouth opened but nothing came out.

"Fine. For now." Brock motioned a soldier to give Jena and Ellis some weapons. "Where to?"

Galin's head jerked towards the grinding gears of the gate opening. He watched his soldiers begin to pour through. He drew his sword. "We take the castle."

"I'm with you," Brock said.

Jena gripped her short sword tightly. "Me, too."

"Me, too. No one kills that goblin-faced toad but me," Ellis said, twirling his new daggers before he slammed them into their sheaths.

"Let's do it!" Galin led the charge towards the castle.

e're going to do it! Galin thought as he charged up the street towards the castle entrance. Just as they cleared the last row of buildings, he stopped. Staerdale Castle was a fortress within a fortress. True, they'd already breached the castle outer walls, but that only led to the nearly abandoned town within the walls.

"Get back here," Brock said as he yanked Galin behind a corner. "They shoot you with an arrow. Don't stand out in the open like that. Are you mad? You're so close, son. Don't blow it."

Galin peered around the corner. Arrows were flying from behind the inner castle walls, embedding themselves into Galin's soldiers. Each scream made his heart race faster. "We've got to do something."

"The air ships?" Jena asked.

"They isn't enough time," Luthur said. "Let me show how we Dwarves handle such shoddy workmanship." He snorted. "They should give us their gold just for putting that weak gate out of its misery."

Ellis smiled. "You know what, Luthur?"

"What?"

"For a fellow who can't see over the bar, you're pretty funny."

Luthur growled. "I'll show you." He stormed off, shouting orders to his fellow Dwarves.

"You shouldn't have done that," Galin said. "He's loyal, and—"

"I know. Sometimes, you need to encourage folks," Ellis said.

"Ellis, you may actually have a brain after all," Jena said.

"Enough of this crap," Brock interrupted. "We have to get through before we lose more of our soldiers to their arrows."

The tingle in Galin's heart grew larger with every beat. He clenched his jaw. But, somehow it was different. It didn't burn or cause great pain. No, it was . . . not like before. Galin closed his eyes, trying to will it away. Nothing. He failed. The tingle became warming and began to spread throughout his body. Was this the Transformation? Yes, it had to be. Jena! He looked into her eyes. Ignoring the falling arrows around them, he pulled her into him and whispered into her ear, "I'm going through the Transformation."

"The what?"

"Soreth said when my power matures, three things could happen. I lose my magic, my power matures like a normal dragon, or it . . . grows beyond my control and I die."

Jena blinked. "No. I won't let you die."

"Die? What the hell are you talking about?" Brock demanded.

Galin ignored him. "I love you. I don't know what will happen, but I'm just happy that I'm spending these moments with you." He passionately kissed her.

Ellis spread them apart. "Please, we've got a war to win."

Galin wiped his mouth. "Where's Luthur?"

"I'm here," Luthur said as he led a battering ram towards Galin.

Galin beamed at the Dwarves' craftsmanship. On top of the battering ram was a hard covering made from dragon scales, hard enough to deflect any arrows or boiling oil. The ram itself was iron, not wood, and it hung in a long swing. Even on dirt, its wheels rolled across the ground like a goose on a pond. "Incredible."

Luthur motioned to the eight Dwarves using the battering ram. "Come on, we've got a door to break down. Go!" He turned toward Galin. "Give them cover."

Galin nodded. "Archers and trebuchets!" As if they'd heard him, arrows and balls of fire flew through the air, beyond the inner castle wall. Galin cringed as screams reached his ears. Yes, they were monsters, but he still felt sorry for them. He looked down at his hand. Tiny little electrical arcs danced along his skin. His power was definitely growing, but would it stop before it consumed him?

Boom! Boom! The dwarves slammed the battering ram into the gate. With each impact, the portcullis bent just a little bit more.

Galin looked up.

Two Feral Orcs hurled large rocks on top of the battering ram, bouncing harmlessly away.

Both orcs screamed as a flaming projectile slammed into that portion of the wall. The timing seemed to be fate. Maybe Odella was cheering for them this day. The wall cracked just above the gate.

The ram slammed into the portcullis again, causing it to buckle. Stones from the archway crumbled to the ground.

Galin kissed Jena. "Let's go!" He raised his sword, pointing at the opening. "Follow me!" Galin ran towards the gate, dodging arrows to his left and his right. He leaped on top of the battering ram and charged beyond it. As soon as his feet hit the ground, an ax swung at his head. He ducked.

The orc raised his ax, bringing it down with all of his might.

Galin tried to roll left, but his tunic got caught under the orc's foot. He looked up to see the blade coming straight for him. The warming turned to rage. The arcs leaped onto his sword, causing it to glow.

The orc screamed.

Galin jumped up. He blinked.

Ellis yanked the dagger from the beast's forehead. "Does being king mean you become stupid, too? Come on, you dumbass."

Thank Odella for Ellis, Galin thought. He smiled as his army rushed by him. Between the inner walls and the castle entrance was a mere one hundred feet, filled with Dark Elves, Feral Orcs, Dwarves, and

Humans, all fighting for their lives. "We've got to find Tanyl and end this."

"They'll be inside," Kade said. "We'll have to push our way to the door. Come on."

"I'm with you, Kade," Brock said.

With his sword brightly glowing, Galin motioned to Ellis and Jena. "Come on." He eyed his first target and swung with all his might.

A Dark Elf batted away Galin's sword. The blue-skinned elf grinned.

Galin recoiled and thrust his sword into the Dark Elf's mid-section.

Two Feral Orcs charged at Jena.

Just before they were going to overtake her, she did a split and sank to the ground. With one fluid motion, she spilled the orcs' intestines on the ground.

Ellis ducked as another arrow nearly took off his head. "You missed!"

The human archer, a mere tens yards from him, nocked another arrow.

"No you don't!" Ellis charged at him with a dagger in each hand. He leaped into the air, tackling the archer. Before his heart took another beat, Ellis slammed both daggers into the human's throat.

Galin slashed another orc, sending it reeling to the ground. He looked down at the orc's cauterized chest. *Even the armor didn't slow my sword down.* Galin looked at the sword his adoptive father had forged for him. Was his dragon magic becoming too powerful?

"There they are!" Kade shouted as he pointed at the entrance. "They run like cowards."

"At least they're not traitors to their own kind," Brock said.

Kade bit his lip.

"Almost there!" Galin shouted. He dodged another ax. Before he could react, Ellis had already taken the Dark Elf down. "Thanks."

"Move it!" Jena yelled. "We've got to get inside." She pushed Galin foreword.

Brock screamed.

Galin spun around. His eyes widened as he saw the sword embedded into Brock's leg.

"No! Not again!" Kade screamed as he charged the three Dark Elves bearing down on Brock to finish the job.

They all swung wildly.

Kade's aged body moved as if he was possessed by Thea the Loyal herself. He parried one to the left. Kade sidestepped and thrust his sword into the mid-section of another.

The third Dark Elf's face nearly went white.

In a single, fluid motion, Kade spun around with his sword in hand, severing the Dark Elf's head from her body. His eyes followed the corpse falling to the ground. He blinked. "Brock." Kade rushed to his side. "Are you all right?" He pulled the sword from Brock's leg, immediately tearing a piece of fabric from his tunic and turning it into a tourniquet around Brock's leg. "You'll be all right." Kade looked up at Galin. "Go, quickly. Get Tanyl and you've won."

"Go with him," Brock said. "He's your nephew. Help him!"

"What about you?" Kade asked.

Luthur pushed Kade aside. "I've got him, you weasel. Now, prove your worth to your family and to yourself. Leave my friend alone."

Kade rose to his feet. "What about the others?"

Luthur winked. "We've got them. Just go. Now!"

Galin extended his hand. "Uncle, let's end this. Let's end this . . . together."

Kade nodded. "They'll be in the Great Hall or somewhere close. You need to watch out for Daylor. He's a powerful mage."

Galin's eyes began to glow a bright sapphire blue. "I know. So was Nyna."

Jena swatted away another Feral Orc ax.

Ellis threw a dagger, slamming it into the beast's skull. "What the hell are we waiting for?"

"Let's go!" Jena said as she ran towards the door.

Galin sighed. "Women." He ran after her.

"WAIT UP!" Galin yelled to Jena.

With her eyes fixed on the hallway ahead and her short sword firmly in her grasp, she stepped back towards Galin. "Coming?"

Galin and Kade rushed to her side with Ellis in tow. "Did you see them?" Galin asked.

Jena shook her head. "No, not yet."

Kade smiled. "Maybe I should lead, since I know where I'm going." He pushed past.

Jena frowned.

The glow from Galin's sword dimmed, but did not vanish completely. "Where's the Great Hall?"

"It's on the other side of the castle," Kade whispered. "We came through the servants' entrance."

"Servants entrance? Figures," Ellis said.

"Quiet!" Galin's grip tightened with each step. He picked up the pace to a fast walk, not quite a run, through the stone corridor. They approached a four-way intersection.

"Left," Kade said.

Galin saw something out of the corner of his right eye. Was it . . . Daylor? He jerked his head to the right, glaring at the traitorous Dark Elf who murdered his mentor. Galin blinked. Daylor's mouth was moving. Was he casting a spell? Galin lowered his shoulder and charged straight at Daylor.

"Guards!" Kade yelled.

Galin looked back for a split-second. Four guards attacked his friends. His sword glowed a bright red. He stopped, with his lead foot skidding towards Daylor. He had to help his friends.

"Galin, watch out!" Jena screamed.

Daylor! Galin tried to regain his balance, but failed. He tumbled into the wall at Daylor's feet, his sword falling to the ground. *Think defense. I must block his attack.*

Three fire bolts appeared over Daylor's shoulder. He smiled. "Good-bye, Galin." As if waiting for his cue, the fire bolts sailed straight at Galin's chest.

Defense! I can do it! Galin reached for his sword. It glowed like it was on fire as soon as he grabbed the hilt.

The three bolts bounced harmlessly off Galin's glowing skin.

Daylor jumped back. "It can't be. You're—" He ran down the corridor.

Galin looked towards his friends; they were still fighting. He could survive Daylor's attacks, but they couldn't. He swallowed. *I have to find him.* He ran after Daylor.

With the clanging of swords behind him, Galin slowed down to a crawl. There was a doorway to the left while the corridor turned to the right. Which way? He shouldn't get too far away from Jena and the others. Perhaps, the door?

Galin pushed the door open with his left hand. Daylor must know that he had taken Galin by surprise, right? Maybe it was another spell? He stepped inside. The kitchen had a huge fireplace at one end with two long work tables in the center of the room. There were at least three wooden blocks filled with knives. Pots and pans hung from the walls. His head turned left and right as if it was on a swivel, scanning everywhere the eyes could see.

"I made a mistake with you," Daylor's voice echoed through the kitchen.

"Where are you? Coward! Is this how you killed Nyna? In hiding?" Galin asked. Daylor's voice appeared to come from across the room, beyond the long tables.

"No. I looked her right in the eyes as she bled out." Daylor laughed. "She couldn't even get a spell out. Amateur."

Where was he? Galin moved to edge of the second long table, peering around the corner. Nothing.

"With all your power, you have to use your eyes to find me?"

Got him! Galin raced along the back wall, towards the fireplace. He must inside it. Invisible, perhaps? Galin swung his sword inside, scraping the hearth with his blade. Nothing. He heard a knife being unsheathed. Galin whirled around. Not one, but eight knives flew out from the knife blocks on the table towards him. Galin dropped to the floor.

The knives flew over him, sticking into the wall.

Daylor screamed as a single knife hit him in the shoulder, pulling him out of invisibility.

Galin leaped at the Dark Elf.

Daylor desperately tried to pull the knife out that had him pinned to the wall. "No!"

Galin dropped his sword to the floor.

"Galin, are you in here?" Kade cried out.

"What are you doing?" Daylor demanded. "Don't kill me."

With fire in his eyes and hatred in his soul, Galin

slammed both hands onto Daylor's chest. He screamed. His skin flashed a dark red. As if the dragon magic pierced Daylor's soul, the Dark Elf's skin dried up. Galin yelled again, focusing all of his energy at the Dark Elf corpse. Daylor's body vaporized.

Galin looked down at his forearms. No burns. No pain. He closed his eyes and opened them again. His skin was back to normal. This was the Transformation. He did not become some monster or lose his power or die. No, he became the first human to truly harness dragon magic. Galin smiled.

"I hope you don't get that pissed at me," Ellis said. He grinned at Kade. "You're screwed."

As soon as Jena entered the kitchen, she ran to Galin. "Are you all right?" Daylor's burning clothes caught her eye. "Did you hurt yourself again? Like before?"

Galin shook his head. "No, I'm fine. The prophecy came true."

Kade grabbed his nephew. "Not yet is hasn't. Let's go."

Galin picked up his sword and led the small group into the corridor.

Tanyl ran up the stairs along the castle's northern side. If he and Chalia raced up and came back down behind the Great Hall, Galin would never find them. As soon as his reinforcements arrived, he would win.

Chalia looked out a window near the top of the stairs. "Sir, look. They're here."

Tanyl smiled. "The Shadow Mage was faster than I thought."

She pointed at an object in the sky. "Is that . . . "

"Yes, their dragon." His hope faded as the necromancers were hit by Soreth's breath weapon. After two strikes, a wave of soldiers overtook them. His reinforcements were no more.

"What now?" she asked.

"We kill Galin and escape. Come on."

"Yes, sir." Chalia followed Tanyl through the door going to the third floor.

"Shouldn't we have at least seen them yet?" Galin asked.

"Yeah," Kade replied. "I've got no idea where they went. If they were going to the Great Hall, we should have seen them."

Galin's grip tightened as he moved down the corridor. He stopped. Sounds of screaming and the clanging of swords and axes grew louder.

"The fighting is in the castle now," Kade said.

"They're getting away," Ellis said. "Let's go already!"

Galin picked up the pace, steadily moving down the corridor.

"There they are! Kill them!" a voice behind them said.

Galin whirled around.

Nine Feral Orcs wearing chain mail armor charged at them. Each was carrying an ax in one hand and a shield in the other.

Ellis sighed. "Shields suck."

Kade raised his sword and charged.

The lead orc effortlessly batted Kade away with his shield. He raised his ax, bringing it down like a guillotine.

Kade screamed.

"Uncle!" Galin cried as he saw Kade's severed hand underneath the orc's ax. His eyes turned red. His skin began to glow. His sword started to glow like fire. With Jena and Ellis at his side, Galin charged in.

The lead orc kicked away Kade's sword, focusing on Galin and the others. He let out a battle cry.

"Screw this," Ellis said. He whipped out a dagger, throwing it down the hallway. It hit its mark. The dagger embedded itself in the orc's right eye. Ellis smiled as the beast crashed to the ground.

Three more orcs jumped forward with their shields out and axes raised.

Galin mustered all the power he could, focusing on their shields. He swung his sword. It cut through two of their shields, but it got stuck in the third.

The middle orc kicked Galin's feet from out from underneath him, sending him crashing to the floor. His sword! He lost his sword!

"No you don't!" Ellis yelled.

Galin watched the ax coming down for his head. He started to roll, but another orc grabbed his legs.

"Galin!" Jena screamed.

Ellis slammed into the orc, stabbing it over and over again with his dagger.

With her short sword above her head and parallel to the ground, Jena leaped over Galin. In midair, she spun round. Her sword was like a natural extension of her arm, severing another orc's head from its body.

An orc grabbed Ellis, slamming him against the wall.

Ellis's eyes widened.

The orc slammed the ax's hilt into the side of Ellis's head, knocking him out. The orc smiled as he dropped Ellis like a sack of onions.

Galin leaped to his feet, yanking his sword from the shield. Jena was fighting another orc. She'd be okay, right? Yeah.

Two more orcs raised their shields.

In a single motion, Galin dropped to the ground and swung his sword underneath their shields, cutting off their legs. As they crashed to the ground. Galin jumped on top of them and finished the job.

"Ellis!" Jena screamed.

Galin whipped around. Ellis was bleeding. His midsection was nicked with an ax. This was not going very well. He looked up at the last two orcs and smiled.

They fled.

Jena was already pulling out her spell components pouch. "I've got to heal them."

Galin nodded. "I'll watch over you."

"No, you'll get Tanyl and end this. I'll not have our baby born into this world when we have a chance to change it." She motioned towards the corridor ahead of them. "As soon as I'm finished, I'll find you.'

Galin said nothing.

"Trust me."

"Okay." Galin bolted down the hall. *I hope I'm doing the right thing.* As he approached a corner, Galin slowed down. Like a cat, he silently peeked around the corner. About twenty yards down the corridor stood orange double doors. There were four Dark Elves in chain mail armor standing guard. *That must be it!* Galin ducked back behind the corner. He could wait until his forces caught up, right? No, he'd risk Tanyl and Chalia getting away and starting this war all over again. It must end tonight!

Galin looked around the corner, just for a second. Too many Dark Elves to knock them out quietly. Could his improved powers make him faster, too? Probably not. Whatever happened, once he stepped beyond the corner he was committed to go right through those doors. He tightened the grip on his sword. Time to find out if that damn prophecy was true. He concentrated. The dragon magic flooded through his body. Galin's skin began to glow and his eyes turned red. He looked down at his hands. This was the Transformation, there was no doubt.

He charged around the corner, directly at the four Dark Elves.

Their eyes widened as Galin's burning-red eyes bore down on them. Three of them raised their swords in defiance, but the forth bolted past Galin, trying to escape.

Galin didn't even turn towards the fleeing Dark Elf. He raised his fiery red sword, letting out a battle cry that nearly shook the castle walls.

The middle elf positioned his sword to parry.

The elves on the either side pulled their swords as if to thrust them into Galin's stomach.

Galin's sword came down like a hammer on an anvil, crashing through the middle Dark Elf's sword, snapping it in two.

The other two Dark Elves thrust towards Galin.

As if anticipating their move, Galin spun while dropping to the ground. His fiery blade sliced through all the Dark Elves. He almost smiled as their torsos separated from their still standing legs. Blood splattered on his face as their bodies collapsed to the ground.

"They're here, you fools!" Tanyl yelled from behind the door. "Chalia, you're a pyromancer, do something!"

Galin looked back towards where Jena should be coming from. Nothing. She wasn't ready or captured or—Damn it! He swallowed. *Think defense.* His reddish skin mutated into a slight purple. Since the Transformation, he hadn't used his defensive abilities. Would they be better or worse? Galin shook his head as he realized that he had no idea what to expect. No, none at all.

"He's coming!" Chalia screamed through the door.

Go! Galin slashed his sword at the doors, slicing them in two like a red-hot knife through a bar of wax. The doors ignited. He kicked what was left of the doors aside. Tanyl was in his sight, not as a captor, but as a soon-to-be victim. With his sword drawn, he moved inside.

"Get him!" Tanyl ordered.

Chalia pointed at Galin and three fiery bolts flew across the room.

Defense! Galin thought. The three bolts bounced harmlessly off his skin. He just smiled at Chalia.

Her blue face whitened. "How?"

"He's using dragon magic, you fool!" Tanyl said as he backed away towards the thrones.

Galin stared directly at the Feral Orcs, who hadn't moved. "Do you know Yotul?"

They shook their heads.

"She's a Feral Orc who joined me. If you surrender to me now, I promise you a new life among us." He pointed at Tanyl. "No one will order you around like slaves. No, you'll be as free as me. No one man or orc or elf or dwarf or gnome is better than any other."

Tanyl laughed. "Really? Feral Orcs are too stupid to understand such platitudes. Besides, you'll never live up to them."

"Do you hear the fighting coming this way?"

They nodded.

"I've already won the day. If you stay with him, you'll die. If you side with me, I'll set your free."

The Feral Orcs looked at each other.

"What are you doing?" Tanyl demanded. "Attack him, you fools!"

"Why?" one of the orcs demanded. "So you can escape while we die? Ever since Methos made us follow the Dark Elves, my people have been fighting and dying for centuries." He stepped forward. "I've had enough."

Chalia pulled a small pouch out from underneath her robes.

"Kogan, please," Tanyl said. "Dark Elves pay the penalty for failure, just like your pitiful kind."

"Who?" Kogan asked.

"Beldroth, to name one. She was a complete failure and damn near destroyed our invasion, which was decades in the making. All she had to do was persuade Galin IV's brother that he needed to start a revolt. That's all. And what did that bitch do? She fell in love with a *human*."

"She was my mother," Chalia whispered.

Tanyl nodded. "Yes, thank Methos you turned out so much better than she did."

"What about all those stories about how she died saving the Darkstriders, ensuring the invasion into

Axain was successful?" A tear rolled down Chalia's right cheek.

"It's a lie. I couldn't let the others know what really happened. It would have caused a revolt," Tanyl said.

"Why lie to me?"

"To keep you under his thumb," Galin said as his skin returned to its normal color. "I never knew your mother."

"You killed my father!" Chalia screamed.

Galin shook his head. "No, he escape from Iron Fist Keep. I don't know where he went." He pointed at Tanyl. "What would Tanyl have done if he made it all the way back here? You know he escaped. You were there, *Mae!*"

Chalia glared at Tanyl. "Is this true?"

Tanyl shrugged. "That I did my duty? Yes, I always do my duty. Don't you?"

Galin's eyes softened.

Chalia backed away.

"Chalia, kill him," Tanyl ordered. "Chalia?" He turned around. She was gone. "Where'd she go?"

Galin shrugged. "She's a mage." *Where did she go? Could her escaping alone ruin everything? No, not anymore, not since she now knew the truth.*

Seven Feral Orcs with axes in hand entered the Great Hall from behind the thrones.

Tanyl smiled. "Finally, I've been stalling these dogs for far too long."

Kogan stepped forward. "You lie to us Orcs." He pointed at Galin. "If we follow the human, he'll free us."

"What do we have to do?" another asked.

"Nothing," Galin said. "I—"

Kogan grinned at Tanyl. "We make the Dark Elf pay for his failure!" With his ax raised high, Kogan and the other Feral Orcs charged.

Tanyl screamed as their axes repeatedly slashed at his body.

Galin stared at the bloody pile of flesh that used to be Tanyl. He sheathed his sword. It was over.

"Galin," Jena said as she ran into the Great Hall. "I —" She covered her mouth as if to hold her stomach contents back when she saw Tanyl's remains. "What happened? Did you?"

Galin shook his head. "No, I didn't."

Kogan stepped forward and knelt before Galin. "Your Majesty, I and my soldiers are at your command."

"Please rise," Galin said. He looked directly at Jena. "Ellis? My uncle?"

She smiled. "They're going to be just fine, as if nothing ever happened to them."

"I love you." He hugged her with all of his heart.

She kissed his cheek. "You need to say something. We've won."

Galin led Jena through the corridors until they reached the courtyard. Bodies littered the ground. The dirt was stained with blood. He looked up as his forces all stared at him.

Tanris knelt down.

One by one, everyone, including Jena, knelt down before him. Galin blushed. "Please, rise." He cleared his throat. "Today will be remembered throughout the history of Axain. It was not just a day when evil was overthrown, but it was also the day when Humans, Elves, Gnomes, Dwarves, and some Feral Orcs all put aside their petty differences and united together. I say, let's not let it end here. As long as I am king, everyone who wants to live peacefully amongst us will be free in our lands." He looked up as Soreth perched on a guard tower and smiled. "Dragons included."

Jena moved next to her husband. "Hail Galin, King of Axain!"

~You did well human, or should I say, little

dragon.~ Soreth said into Galin's mind. He smiled, then flew off into the distance.

Galin raised his arms, silencing the crowds. "My adoptive father told me that a single female knight in Axain, Thea the Loyal, sacrificed herself in order to save the kingdom. From this day forward, we will feast in her honor."

The crowd cheered.

He looked into Jena's eyes. "I wish Sally and Keya could see us."

Jena looked up at the sky. "They can. I know they can."

Galin pulled her in close. "I'll never let anything happen to you." He kissed her.

"I love you too, Galin."

"WHAT IS TAKING SO LONG?" Galin demanded as he paced back and forth in front of the thrones. He adjusted the thin gold crown on his head. The royal robes of Axain seemed to float in the air behind him. It has been seven months after they defeated the Darkstriders and he still couldn't sit quietly on his throne. Well, not when waiting for something important.

"You're like your father, when you were born," Kade chuckled.

Ellis burst into the Great Hall. "Did she have him yet?"

"Him?" Galin asked. "How do you know?"

"Well—I assumed." Ellis shrugged. "Sorry."

"It won't be long, son," Brock said. "I promise."

The small door behind the thrones burst open. The nanny raced inside, carrying a baby.

"Is it?" Galin asked.

She nodded. "It's a girl."

Galin took the precious treasure from the old woman. He looked into his daughter's hazel eyes. "She looks like her mother."

"Will she be your heir?" the woman asked.

Galin looked up.

Kade shook his head. "Only the firstborn male child can be king."

"Why? Why is that? Why can a king rule better than a queen?"

"I—well—it's tradition," Kade said.

Galin looked down at his daughter. She smiled at him. "No, our firstborn child will rule." He kissed her forehead. As soon as his lips touched her head he felt—something. He looked directly into her eyes.

The hazel eyes flashed red, just for a second, then returned to normal.

"Why break with tradition?" Kade asked.

Galin grinned. "Because this one is very special indeed. Maybe more special than her father."

"Sire," the nanny began, "the queen."

"Right." Galin looked towards his family and friends. "I need to attend to the queen."

"Seems like old times," Kade said as he slapped Brock on the shoulder.

Brock nodded. "Yeah, we've come *full circle.*"

"I love you all." Galin and the baby rushed behind the thrones to see Jena.

Hi, I'm Steven Atwood. I grew up reading fantasy books and watching science fiction whenever I could. When I was young, I played role-playing games within the fantasy genre. Close to the end of my military career, I started to write. It was something I always wanted to do but never did. I write science fiction and fantasy with a fresh perspective.

Visit my website

http://stevenatwood.net

facebook.com/stevenatwoodauthor
twitter.com/SteAtwood
bookbub.com/profile/steven-atwood
instagram.com/steven_atwood_author

Science Fiction

Cyber Invasion

Amari

Nano WMD

Fantasy

Prophecy of Axain Series, 2nd Edition

Prophecy of Axain

Iron Fist Keep

Full Circle

Box Sets

Prophecy of Axain Boxset